STAMPEDE!

One of the horses reared. The one next to it bucked, kicking another horse who bit the one who had reared. Every horse whose ears hadn't flattened before now flattened its ears, and they all started whinnying and crying wildly.

Two more horses reared, and that was all the rest of the herd would take. They fled.

Stevie and Kate stood helplessly by the open gate while more than a dozen horses raced past them right into the middle of the herd of cattle.

The cattle, which had been just as restless as the horses, found this an ideal opportunity to run. Within a matter of seconds it was clear to Stevie and Kate that they had a full-blown stampede on their hands.

"Eli!!!" Stevie shrieked.

THE SADDLE CLUB

Ranch Hands

Bonnie Bryant

A BANTAM SKYLARK BOOK®
NEW YORK · TORONTO · LONDON · SYDNEY · AUCKLAND

RL 5, 009–012

RANCH HANDS

A Bantam Skylark Book / August 1993

Skylark Books is a registered trademark of Bantam Books,
a division of Bantam Doubleday Dell Publishing Group, Inc.
Registered in U.S. Patent and Trademark Office and elsewhere.

"The Saddle Club" is a trademark of Bonnie Bryant Hiller.
The Saddle Club design / logo, which consists of an inverted
U-shaped design, a riding crop, and a riding hat is a
trademark of Bantam Books.

ISBN 0-553-48076-6

Published simultaneously in the United States and Canada

Bantam Books are published by Bantam Books, a division of Bantam
Doubleday Dell Publishing Group, Inc. Its trademark, consisting of the
words "Bantam Books" and the portrayal of a rooster, is Registered in
U.S. Patent and Trademark Office and in other countries. Marca Regis-
trada. Bantam Books, 1540 Broadway, New York, New York 10036.

PRINTED IN THE UNITED STATES OF AMERICA

OPM   0   9   8   7   6   5   4   3   2   1

For Susan Korman—if she'll have it

B.B.

"I've got a secret," Carole Hanson said to Lisa Atwood.

"Oh, no, I don't like secrets at all," Lisa complained.

"But I always thought you *loved* secrets!" Carole said. The two of them were walking to their favorite place, Pine Hollow Stables, to meet their friend Stevie Lake and celebrate the fact that school was out for the summer. Carole couldn't think of any good reason to be upset about anything, especially secrets.

"Usually I like secrets, but not right now. It's my parents," Lisa continued. "They've been tiptoeing around the house and whispering to each other for days. Something's up. It's a secret, and I have the funniest feeling that I'm not going to like it."

"Don't be such a pessimist," Carole said. "And don't blame me for your parents' secret. I promise you're going to like mine."

"Then it must have to do with horses," said Lisa.

"Maybe," Carole said. "But I can't tell it to you until we meet up with Stevie."

Carole was being a lot more mysterious than usual. Normally Stevie was the one who was good at mysteries and secrets—especially the part about *telling* secrets. She wasn't nearly as good at keeping them.

The three best friends, Stevie, Carole, and Lisa, were very different from one another, but they all felt the same way about horses. They loved horses so much that they had formed their own club and called it The Saddle Club. The first requirement for membership was that the members had to be horse crazy. That was easy for Carole, Stevie, and Lisa, who were totally horse crazy. The second requirement was that each member had to be willing to help out another member whenever she needed it. Sometimes the help had to do with horses. Sometimes it had to do with other things—like schoolwork, parents, or boyfriends. Judging by the look on Lisa's face, Carole had the funny feeling she and Stevie might soon be pitching in to help Lisa cope with her parents' secret. Since there was nothing to be done about that for the moment, Carole's thoughts turned to a more pleasant subject.

"I think I want to try to ride every day this summer," she said.

"That's my favorite part about summer," Lisa said, nodding in agreement. "As long as Max will let us, we *can* ride every day."

Max was the owner of Pine Hollow. Since he knew what good riders Stevie and Lisa were, he let them ride as long as their horses weren't being used in a riding class. That didn't apply to Carole, though. She owned her own horse and could ride Starlight any time she wanted. In fact, she really had to ride him— or see that he got exercise one way or another—almost every day. That was fine with Carole. She was never happier than when she was with Starlight.

"If I can ride every day," Lisa went on, "imagine how much better a rider I'll be when fall comes again. I particularly want to work on my jumping."

"Riding isn't the only important part about horses," Carole reminded her. "There's a lot of work to be done on horse care, too."

"I know, and stable management and all sorts of other things that have to be done before you get on the horse's back. Those things are hard, but fun. Know what I mean?"

"I do," Carole agreed.

The two of them chatted about all the things they wanted to do at Pine Hollow in the next two months as they walked there together. It was a hot day, promising more of the same as the summer wore on. They lived in the town of Willow Creek, Virginia, about twenty miles outside Washington, D.C., and the area was noted for its muggy summer weather. The girls never minded, though, as long as they could be with their horses.

Stevie was standing out in front of the stable, waiting for them.

"Come on, girls," she said. "There isn't a minute to waste. We have exactly two months and eight days until school starts. That means sixty-eight straight days of riding—or is it sixty-nine? Thirty days hath September . . ."

"Oh, stop wasting time counting," Lisa said. She knew Stevie would never remember the jingle correctly, and it might take a while to figure out the answer to the question. She thought there was something much more important to do with their time. "Let's just ride!" She marched toward the locker area in the stable.

"Okay," Stevie said agreeably, following Lisa inside. She couldn't remember whether it was April or July that had thirty days anyway.

"Not quite so fast," Carole said. "I've still got this secret."

That stopped Stevie in her tracks. "Yes?" she asked expectantly.

"Well, let's get to the locker area and then I'll show

you. It's very hard to read a letter from a friend if I'm walking around at the same time."

That gave it away for Stevie. "Kate?" she asked.

Carole grinned and nodded.

"Then let's hurry up and sit down!"

Kate Devine was a friend of all three girls. They had originally met her because her father had been an officer in the Marine Corps with Carole's father. When Kate's father had retired, he'd bought a dude ranch out West, and the girls had visited Kate there and learned a whole lot about a new kind of riding.

Kate, herself, was an excellent rider. In fact, she'd been a junior national champion, but she'd stopped riding competitively when she found that beating others had become the most important factor in riding. It took meeting up with The Saddle Club to get her back on a horse, and she'd never been sorry. Now she got to ride all the time and never competed a bit—except with the dudes who came to stay at her family ranch.

Lisa and Stevie stowed their street shoes and pulled on their boots while Carole opened the letter. She sat down on the bench and began to read out loud. With every word, Lisa and Stevie slowed down the dressing process. They had to sit still to take in all the good news. First of all, Kate told them that Eli and Jeannie had gotten married. Eli used to be the head wrangler at the Devines' dude ranch, and Jeannie had worked there as well. The girls had even helped get the two of them together, because Eli had been a little blind about how much Jeannie liked him. Then, when Eli had gone away to school, Jeannie had followed him there. It seemed very right that they'd finally gotten married.

"A complete riding club and matchmaking service —that's us!" Stevie announced proudly. Lisa agreed, but she shushed Stevie up anyway. She wanted to hear the rest of the letter.

> Eli and Jeannie have rented a ranch in Wyoming for the summer and they want to run a summer camp for kids there. Most of the kids who have signed up are younger than we are. Eli called Dad last week and asked if Dad knew any riders who might like to come. He said he was hoping to find some really good riders who would both be able to have fun and to help the younger kids. He said he's going to need a lot of help and that it will be work so he's got to have good, reliable riders. He kept saying things like he hoped to find people with different kinds of riding skills—even English. Of course, he was just fishing. He meant me and you three. So? What do you think? It's for three weeks. It would be pretty hard work because it's not just a ranch, it's a farm, too, so we'd be kind of living off the land. Dad says I can go. He says

we can even pick you guys up in the plane—and bring you home again. We'll come get you. Just give the word!

"Yes!" Stevie said, almost breathlessly.

"Yes, yes!" Carole added.

"Make that three!" said Lisa.

Then Carole passed around the brochure that Eli and Jeannie had sent Kate. It showed photographs of breathtakingly beautiful scenery on the edge of the Rocky Mountains. The ranch was nestled in a valley, and a sign showed its name as High Meadow.

One look and Stevie knew she had to go. She could almost see herself mounted on a pinto pony standing beneath the sign that stretched between the two posts at the gate of the ranch.

She was torn then. She wanted to run home and begin the process of talking her parents into letting her go. But then, she also wanted to stay at Pine Hollow and go for a ride with Lisa and Carole. Of course, she decided to stick around for the ride. Besides, her parents were both at work and wouldn't be home until dinnertime.

"Just imagine!" Lisa said. "Eli wants *us* to help with his riders."

"Not just *wants*," Carole said. "He *needs* us."

"I guess there are advantages to being pretty good

on a horse," said Stevie. "And this is definitely one of them. Why, we'll practically be camp counselors."

"That's no surprise," said Carole. "We're good enough riders, aren't we?"

"It's not just the riding," Lisa added. "It's all the other things we can do, too, like grooming and feeding. Eli and Jeannie really know they can rely on us."

That gave all the girls a wonderful feeling. They loved riding and taking care of horses. They also liked the fact that somebody else recognized and valued their skills.

Stevie gave her boot a final tug and then stood up. "Let's go," she said. "And let's play a game—pretending we're already at High Meadow. I'll be an obstreperous little kid, and you two can teach me everything you know. . . ."

Since Stevie was very good at being obstreperous (a word she heard frequently from the headmistress of her school), the game promised to be a fun one. Carole and Lisa stood up eagerly.

Just then, though, Mrs. Reg entered the locker area. Mrs. Reg was Max's mother and the stable manager. She always seemed to know absolutely everything that was going on everywhere. Lisa often suspected she had a pair of antennae hidden beneath her soft gray hair.

"Topside has already taken two classes today," Mrs. Reg said to Stevie. "You can take him out on the trail, but only if you'll be back within an hour and don't ride him too hard."

"It's too hot to ride him hard," Stevie agreed. "I'd never do that. And we'll definitely be back within an hour. We've got something important to do."

"Yes, I'm sure," said Mrs. Reg. "You know, though, that reminds me of something. . . ."

The three girls each sighed silently. Then, one by one, they sat down. Whenever Mrs. Reg said that, it meant she was about to tell them a story. Her stories always had to do with horses and often didn't seem connected with whatever it was she'd been reminded of. More often, they were connected with something else that was going on, and it became a challenge to the young riders to figure out exactly *how* they were connected to what was going on. This one was no exception.

"There was a young boy who used to ride at Pine Hollow," she began. She told about this boy—whom she never named—and how he'd loved horses and speed. It seemed that he wanted, more than anything, to grow up to be a jockey. He spent all his free time at the racetrack and hung around with the jockeys, wanting more than anything to be just like them.

When he became a teenager, though, it became clear that he would never get his wish, for he began to grow. A lot.

"He was over six feet by the time he stopped. And

big boned, too. He looked more like a wrestler than a jockey."

The girls knew that successful jockeys were all very small people, usually just over five feet and about a hundred pounds. The lighter the jockey, the easier it was for the horse to run quickly.

"For a long time, he was very sad," said Mrs. Reg. Then she stopped and looked off into the middle distance, sort of dreamily. It was just like her to stop when a story seemed to be getting interesting. Sometimes, if she were prodded in just the right way, she'd continue and give a hint as to what she was talking about.

"Then what happened?" Lisa asked.

Mrs. Reg looked puzzled, as if she couldn't figure out why Lisa didn't know the answer. "Are you girls going to go on your ride, or are you going to lollygag around here all afternoon? I've got work to do, you know. . . ." With that she left, leaving the girls to unravel the meaning of the story.

Stevie thought she knew the right question. "What made him stop being sad?" she asked. She looked at Carole and Lisa.

"I think I know," Carole said. "I think she's talking about Mr. McLeod, the trainer who owned Prancer." Prancer was a mare who now belonged to Pine Hollow. She had been bred as a racehorse but had to retire from the track because of an injury. Then she'd been moved to Pine Hollow, where she began her stable horse career. "See, when he couldn't become a jockey, he became a trainer; and he's still a trainer today."

"Is that bad?" Lisa asked.

"I don't think so," Carole said. "He seemed like a very happy man when I met him. And if he'd become a jockey, he probably would have had to retire by now."

"Of course he's happy. He's working with horses," Lisa said, totally logical. She figured anybody who could spend all day every day around horses had to be a happy person.

"I think I've got it then," said Stevie. That meant that she'd figured out what it was Mrs. Reg had been trying to tell them. Her stories always had a meaning. Deciphering that meaning wasn't always so easy. "Mr. McLeod didn't get exactly what he wanted, but he got something just as good, maybe even better."

"Makes sense to me," Lisa agreed.

"Getting on the trail makes even more sense," Carole said.

That was an idea that didn't have to be deciphered. The girls quickly tacked up their horses and headed for the woods. The first day of summer vacation had to be properly celebrated.

CAROLE'S FATHER WAS late coming home from his office on the nearby Marine Corps base. Carole was so nervous about asking him if she could go to Eli's ranch for the summer that she couldn't stop fidgeting. She decided a bribe couldn't hurt her cause and began preparing dinner for the two of them.

The problem was, Carole could be a little flaky and scatterbrained—except when it came to horses, of course. That was why she put the frozen green beans in the frying pan and the hamburgers got dunked in the salted water. Fortunately, the baked potatoes didn't suffer from being put in the refrigerator, and neither did they get cooked there.

By the time her father got home, the slightly soggy hamburgers were frying and the slightly crisped green beans were boiling. The potatoes, now thoroughly chilled, were rescued from the refrigerator and hastily tucked into the microwave where she cooked them until they were very wrinkly.

"How nice!" Colonel Hanson said, looking at the meal that appeared in front of him. He smiled eagerly. "Is this what I have to look forward to now that school is out for the summer, home-cooked meals every night?"

"More like 'home-ruined' meals every night, you mean, and maybe I'll alternate it with 'home-burned' some nights," Carole said despondently. She took a bite out of the hamburger and grimaced.

Colonel Hanson tried the browned beans. Then he turned his attention to the potato. The news wasn't any better.

"Let me show you an old cook's trick," Colonel Hanson said. He picked up his plate and Carole's and took them over to the counter.

"This is the beginner chef's most valuable tool," he said. And with a flourish, he picked up the telephone and ordered a pizza for the two of them: pepperoni, green pepper, onions, and mushrooms. It would arrive in a half hour.

Carole was hungry, and the pizza sounded awfully good to her, but it wasn't what she'd had in mind. She apologized to her father for messing up the dinner and even told him how she'd done it.

"Oh, don't worry about it," he assured her. "I've boiled more hamburgers than I care to remember— although I think one boiled hamburger qualifies as more than I care to remember." The corners of his mouth twitched a little as he tried to suppress a chuckle. It didn't work. He couldn't hold it in. He started laughing. Carole couldn't help herself. She started laughing, too.

"I was just trying to do something nice," she said. Then she scraped her failed dinner into the garbage. Her father did the same.

"I know, honey. It was nice, too. At least the *idea* was nice. What I'm wondering, though, is what was distracting you so badly that you boiled the hamburgers?"

"And fried the beans and chilled the potatoes," she reminded him. He nodded. "Well," she began. "I got a letter from Kate . . ."

"Eli's ranch?" Colonel Hanson asked.

"You know about it?"

"Frank Devine called me this afternoon," he said. "He told me that Eli's hoping to get some real work out of you girls. I told him I wasn't sure you'd want to spend the whole time working with horses, feeding, grooming, riding, instructing—not when there was a chance to go to cooking school. . . ."

"Dad!"

Colonel Hanson knew when to stop teasing, too.

14

"Actually, Carole, it's perfect," he said. "I got word yesterday from our commanding officer at the base that I'm going to have to go on an extended inspection tour. I knew I could take you along, but I also knew you would have been bored to tears. So, of course I told Frank it was okay by me if you went to Eli's ranch—that is, if I could talk you into it."

"Just try me," she said, unable to hide her grin of utter joy. She was going to the ranch!

They spent the next hour eating every bit of the delicious and perfectly cooked pizza and talking about Carole's summer on the ranch. They had a wonderful time, and in the end Carole concluded that the only bad thing about going to Eli's ranch was that she really was going to miss her dad.

LISA PULLED HER chair into the table and put her napkin on her lap. She'd spent the last hour in her room trying to figure out how to talk her parents into letting her go to Eli's ranch. It wasn't going to be an easy job, but she was sure she could manage it. The strongest point would be that Eli was expecting the girls to work. It really was more of a summer job than a summer camp. Eli needed their help, and it was going to be a real work experience. "Imagine how that will look on my college applications!" she'd say. She figured her parents would love that.

She had also decided that she should bring it up early in the meal—as soon as the last plate was served.

Lisa's mother nodded to Mr. Atwood, who began to serve. He finished his wife's plate and passed it to her. *One down, two to go,* Lisa told herself. He put the food on her plate and handed it to her. "Thank you," she said out loud. *Two down, one to go,* she said to herself.

"Lisa, we've got some wonderful news for you," her mother said.

"We sure do!" said her father, putting his own plate down in front of himself. *Three down . . .*

"You tell," said Mrs. Atwood.

"No, *you* do it," said Mr. Atwood.

And so she did. Lisa's mother told her that the three of them were going to Europe for a full month! They were going to leave in two weeks. They would go to England, France, and Italy. They would see everything! Her parents had been planning this trip to be a surprise for her for months.

"We started planning it right after Christmas," her father said.

"We know you're going to love it!"

Lisa listened. She was too stunned even to speak. All her life, she'd dreamed of the day she might take a trip to Europe, but not now. Not *this* summer when she could go to the ranch with Carole and Stevie. Not when she could spend the summer riding Western ponies and being a real hand on a real ranch, helping Eli

16

and teaching little kids. Not when something else so wonderful was going on.

"Isn't it exciting?" Her mother's face positively glowed with excitement. Lisa nodded numbly.

"We knew you'd be surprised," said Mr. Atwood. "And we wanted it to be a surprise, too. You can't imagine how hard it's been. . . ."

Lisa's father began a long explanation about how the phone call Lisa thought was a wrong number the other day had actually been the travel agent. Lisa barely heard the story. All she really heard was Europe and four weeks. She'd even be gone before her friends would leave for Eli's. She'd be in places where they didn't have horses, where they couldn't ride every day. She'd even be in places where they didn't speak English and didn't know her and she didn't know anybody. She wouldn't have any friends around, just her parents.

Lisa looked at the two of them. They'd seen the blank look on her face and took it to be excitement. Lisa was glad of that. She loved her parents. She couldn't disappoint them when they had gone to so much trouble for her.

". . . the Eiffel Tower and the Louvre. And don't forget Nôtre Dame. I read that there's a boat trip you can take on the Seine through the city. They call it The City of Lights, you know. . . ."

The City of Lights—a place she'd never been, filled with strange people, strange foods, strange words. What did it hold for her? Not much, Lisa thought. She wanted to go to the ranch. She wanted to ride and be with her friends.

She had to try to tell her parents. She took a deep breath and interrupted an explanation about the ceiling of the Sistine Chapel.

"Kate Devine's invited us all to go to a Western riding camp that Eli's running this summer. It's called High Meadow. We'd be working—"

"No work for you this summer. Just pleasure!" her mother interrupted.

The ranch trip was dead and Lisa knew it. She was going to Europe with her parents.

She felt totally overwhelmed. She couldn't even take a bite of the meat loaf. She just put down her fork. She had to be alone. She wanted to cry, and she didn't want her parents to know how disappointed she was.

"Excuse me," she said. She stood up from the table and headed for her room as quickly as she could.

"She's going to call her friends and give them the good news," she heard her mother say to her father.

The tears welled up in Lisa's eyes. The *terrible* news she silently corrected her mother.

* * *

A PEA FLEW across the table and hit Stevie squarely on the forehead. She stuck her tongue out at her twin brother, Alex.

"Stop that!" Mrs. Lake said to Stevie.

"He threw the pea at me!" Stevie protested.

"What *are* you talking about?" Alex asked sweetly. "Of course I didn't throw a pea at you—though, of course, I might have if I'd thought of it, because a certain sister of mine is a total dirty rotten fink."

Stevie knew what he was talking about, but she didn't agree that she'd been rotten. After all, if Alex actually liked Melissa Sanders and thought she was cute, what was wrong with Stevie letting Melissa know it? How could she have anticipated that Melissa would then post a large, public note on Alex's locker saying she wouldn't go out with him if he were the last boy on earth. Stevie hardly thought she should be held responsible for that. It was Alex's poor taste in girlfriends that brought it on, not her telling Melissa that Alex thought she was cute.

"I'm going to get you," Alex said. "Every day this summer I'm going to hide by the trails at that precious stable and scare your horse as you ride by."

Stevie sneered. "Shows how much you know," she said. "I won't be here this summer."

There was a silence at the table.

"Just where do you plan to be?" Mrs. Lake asked.

"Out West," she said. "See, Eli is running this Western riding camp, and he's asked The Saddle Club to come help him. We're going to be like junior counselors."

"No," her parents said in a single voice. That surprised Stevie just a little bit. Normally, it took a few seconds for them to veto one of her plans.

". . . and maybe some days I'll put a burr under your horse's saddle," Alex continued, totally ignoring Stevie's announcement. "And it seems to me that your friend, Phil, ought to know that you wrote his name one hundred times in your history notebook. And then there were the other doodles . . ."

Phil was Stevie's boyfriend. She'd met him at riding camp. He had two sisters who teased him as much as Stevie's three brothers teased her, so he was pretty understanding when Stevie's brothers gave him a hard time. She really didn't want him to know about her history notebook, though. She blushed just thinking about it. Then she took more direct action. She threw a pea at Alex.

"Stevie!" her mother said sternly.

"Alex!" Mr. Lake scowled.

Pretty soon Stevie's other brothers joined in the fray. It wasn't clear who was taking which side. It was only clear that there was loud accusatory shouting going on.

Stevie yelled at Alex, but she was also keeping an

eye on her parents because she noticed that they'd exchanged a look.

"You know," Mrs. Lake said to Mr. Lake, ducking a flying pea, "maybe a month out West would be a nice change for Stevie. . . ."

And that was how Stevie found out that she was Westward bound.

3

THERE WAS SO much to do and so little time to do it. Lisa hurried out of her mother's car and darted through the crowd at the mall. She was meeting Stevie and Carole for a final Saddle Club meeting before she left for Europe.

It still hurt to know that she wouldn't spend the summer at High Meadow with her friends. It had taken her two days to be able to tell them. As it turned out, they'd all cried. It was a funny cry, too, because although Lisa was terribly disappointed not to be going to High Meadow, there was a part of her that was excited about going to Europe.

"They do have horses in Europe," Stevie had reminded her.

"Not at the Cathedral of Nôtre Dame in Paris," Lisa said.

"Well, the Queen of England rides a lot," Stevie said, trying desperately to find a bright side.

"Yeah, and I'm sure to be invited for a hack with her in Hyde Park, too."

"You never know," said Carole, joining in on the cheering-up work.

"Oh, yes, I do," said Lisa.

Of course her friends knew she was right.

The Saddle Club had only one more day together, and they needed to spend it at the mall—not that they minded. Each of them had a shopping list of essential items for the summer. And they could stop and have a sundae when they were done. That would be their farewell Saddle Club meeting.

Lisa stood on tiptoe, looking over the crowd for her friends. She spotted them easily because Stevie was waving frantically. Another giveaway was the fact that Stevie and Carole were stationed in front of Riding Togs. Naturally, it was their favorite store.

Stevie greeted Lisa with a brief hug and the announcement that Riding Togs was having a sale on cowboy hats.

"Come on in. Help us choose!" Lisa followed gladly.

They found Carole trying on an oversized black felt hat with a silver band.

"I don't think it's you," Lisa said mildly.

"Definitely not, but isn't it hysterical?" she asked, her eyes sparkling.

Lisa nodded and then glanced at the selection. She was a logical thinker, and her sense of logic made her eliminate the impossible options: hats that were too big or too bizarre. It didn't take her long to narrow down the selection.

"Here, this tan one for you, Carole. And Stevie, I think you should go with a black. It'll bring out the light colors in your hazel eyes."

Both Carole and Stevie took Lisa's suggestions. They were tempted to buy the hats without even trying them on because Lisa was so convincing, but they did slip them onto their heads and agreed that Lisa knew what she was talking about.

"Now to kerchiefs," Stevie said.

Once they'd chosen their hats, the rest was easy. They both needed riding jeans, meaning jeans without a seam on the inside of the leg. It was much more comfortable in the saddle that way. Stevie treated herself to two kerchiefs despite Carole's saying she looked as if she were about to rob a bank when she pulled one of them up over her nose.

"It's to keep the dust out of my mouth," Stevie said. "Remember how dry and dusty the trails get?" Carole did remember. That inspired her to buy herself a couple of kerchiefs, too.

After Riding Togs, it was Lisa's turn. She wanted to go to the bookstore.

"I've got to get books about French and Italian. They don't speak English there, you know. . . ."

"There are some people who say they don't speak it in England, either," Stevie teased.

Lisa laughed and then browsed through the foreign language section. "Arabic, Catalan, Chinese, Danish. . . . Boy, there certainly are a lot of languages I don't know. It's sort of overwhelming."

The minute she said the word, she felt the feeling: overwhelming. It was frightening to her. Stevie seemed to sense that she needed some reassurance. That was one of the nice things about Stevie.

"Oh, don't worry," she said. "You've been studying French. You'll have the phrase books. And don't forget, a lot of the people over there speak perfectly good English, too."

"Name one," Lisa said glumly.

"I'll name four," Carole chirped in. "Remember the Italian boys?"

Lisa did, of course. Four Italian riders had come to Pine Hollow to do a demonstration of their riding skills as part of an international Pony Club exchange program. They'd all been wonderful riders, which the girls had expected; they'd also spoken excellent English. And, best of all, they'd been really nice guys.

"Right!" Lisa said, cheering up with the thought. "Maybe I'll run into them."

"Sure," said Stevie. "I'm positive all of their parents will have just decided to drag them all over every tourist spot in Rome, and you'll definitely be there at the same time. I bet they've never been to St. Peter's before, and this is the time they'll do it."

Lisa got the point. She and her parents were going to be at all the main tourist attractions, hardly the places where she'd expect to run into their friends. Still, it made her feel better just thinking about the boys. They'd been so nice that she became more confident that the other people they'd meet there would be nice, too.

"Here's just the thing for you," Stevie said, pulling another book off the shelf and handing it to Lisa.

"British English for Americans," she said, reading the title out loud.

Lisa flipped the book open.

" 'Smashing,' " she read. "Says here it doesn't have anything to do with crumpling or breaking anything up. It means 'totally awesome.' " She made a face. "I think I could have figured that out."

Stevie took the book and glanced at a page. "Sure, everybody knows about 'smashing,' but do you know what 'bangers and mash' are?"

"What?"

" 'Bangers and mash,' " Stevie said smugly. "That

means sausages and mashed potatoes. If you're not careful and don't watch what you're doing, you could get that in a restaurant."

"Don't worry," Lisa assured her. "I would *never* order something called 'bangers and mash.' "

Stevie put the book back on the shelf, and the three girls made their way to the cash register where Lisa paid for her books.

"Next?" Carole asked.

"A stationery store," Lisa said. "If I can't be with you guys and talk to you and ride with you, the very least I can do is to write you loads of letters."

"But we won't be able to write you back," said Carole. "You and your parents will be moving around so much we won't know where to find you."

"Then you're just going to have to keep a diary and let me read it when I get back. It'll be like three weeks' worth of letters all at once."

Stevie thought that keeping a diary sounded like something one of her teachers would suggest to her— the sort of thing that might be a makeup assignment for time off from school.

"No thanks," she said. "I'm not really good at doing things regularly like that. I'm not the reliable, organized one. That's you."

"I'll keep a diary," Carole volunteered. Although she wasn't writing in one now, Carole had used a diary before. She'd kept a diary when her mother was ill and found it was a wonderful source of memories for her. She thought if she kept a diary while she and Stevie were at High Meadow, that could be a wonderful source of memories for Lisa. "I think it's a good idea. I'll even get one without a lock so you can look at it any time."

Lisa pored over the stationery, finally selecting some pink paper with flower-lined envelopes. Carole chose a no-nonsense diary, a plain, leather-covered book with lots and lots of lined pages. She also bought one for Stevie, just in case she changed her mind.

While Carole and Lisa were busy making their selections, Stevie chose a pen for Lisa as a farewell present. It had scented ink.

"It says it's 'balsam,' " Stevie explained when Lisa joined up with her at the cash register. "Personally, I think it smells like a pine tree, and that's to remind you of Pine Hollow."

It was just like Stevie to do something so little and so wonderful. For a minute, Lisa thought she might start crying again.

"No you don't," Carole said, spotting the redness in her eyes. "You're going to have a wonderful summer, and even if it's not exactly what we had in mind, it'll still be fun. And, remember, if you're away from us for four weeks, that means four weeks of not having to watch Stevie eat the kind of thing she's about to eat!"

Stevie's eyes lit up. "Is it sundae time?"

"I think so," Carole said, glancing at her watch.

The girls usually went to an ice cream parlor they called TD's because it was close to Pine Hollow. There wasn't a branch of TD's at the mall, but there was an ice cream shop that was almost as good.

It only took the girls a few minutes to settle into a booth. A waitress arrived promptly and took their orders. For Lisa, it was a vanilla frozen yogurt with some granola on top. Carole wanted a plain hot fudge sundae. As usual, Stevie's order was a little more unusual.

"Have you got that praline cream flavor?" she asked. The waitress told her they did. "Good, then I'll have that." The waitress turned to leave. "But I'd like something on it." The waitress came back to the table. Her eyes searched Stevie's face.

"Haven't I seen you here before?"

"Maybe," Stevie said.

"What would you like with the praline cream?" the waitress asked.

"A scoop of raspberry swirl, topped with Butterfingers' crunch and blueberry cheesecake crumble."

The waitress had to work very hard to keep a straight face, but she wrote everything down carefully and repeated it back to Stevie.

"Is that right?" she asked.

"Perfect," Stevie said.

"Yes, I definitely have seen you before," the woman

said. "I may forget a face, but I *never* forget an order, especially the kind you like. Ugh!"

With that, she left the girls alone. Lisa and Carole were trying unsuccessfully to stifle their giggles. Stevie didn't seem to understand what the fuss was about. That made Lisa and Carole laugh even harder.

It was a bittersweet Saddle Club meeting, and Lisa was both sad and relieved when it was over. For one thing, she didn't want to stop being with her friends, swapping tales, talking about horses, and just hanging out. For another, though, it was hard being with them when she knew that, as of the next morning, she wouldn't be seeing them for so long. Good-byes were hard—especially when they had to last for four long weeks.

Stevie's mother picked the girls up at the mall and dropped them off at their homes, Carole first, then Lisa. As Lisa walked toward her front door, she didn't think she could stand to hear the word good-bye one more time.

She shifted her package to her other arm, recalling as she did that it was filled with foreign words and phrases. The very next day she would be on her way to Europe. She knew that it was the trip of a lifetime —and there was a part of her that was excited about it. But there was also a part of her that was sad about it. And another part that was very frightened. Europe was very far away and very different from America.

STEVIE LOOKED OUT the rear window of her parents' station wagon as they drove toward the airport. She was lying on top of three duffel bags, and Carole lay next to her. Stevie was glad she'd packed so many clothes since her duffel bag was nice and soft. Carole's, on the other hand, had riding boots prominently bulging.

Stevie's father and Colonel Hanson were in the front seat. Stevie's younger brother, Michael, sat between them. Stevie's mother and her other two brothers were in the rear seat. Stevie thought it took an awful lot of people to say good-bye to two girls.

"Lisa was here day before yesterday," Carole said, interrupting Stevie's thoughts.

"And now she's in Paris," Stevie said. "I wish she were here, don't you?"

"Of course, but I bet she'll have fun on her trip, anyway."

"More fun than we'll have?"

"No way. But fun, anyway," Carole replied.

Stevie knew Carole was right. Lisa wasn't thrilled about her vacation, but how bad could it be, going to France, England, and Italy? The *only* thing missing was horses. And friends.

"You've got a funny look on your face," Carole said. "Do you wish we were flying to Paris instead of Wyoming?"

"For a second I did," Stevie answered truthfully. "It would be a wonderful trip."

"So will ours," Carole promised.

"Right. And you know what I really love about what we're going to do? It's the fact that Eli and Jeannie are counting on us to be helpers, not just campers. We'll be like counselors."

"Sure, we'll be teaching the other kids things about horses and riding."

"And they'll do what we tell them to do," Stevie added.

From the seat in front of them, Mrs. Lake started laughing. Stevie asked her what she was laughing about.

"It's about those kids who will do what you tell them to do," she said. "They'll probably be as good at that as you are!" She was teasing, and Stevie knew it, but it made her stop and think.

"Of course they will," Carole said. "It's because what we'll be telling them will be about horses, and they're going to want to learn, just the way we always do."

Carole's father turned around from the front seat. "Does that mean you always do what Max tells you?"

"Always," Stevie assured him.

Carole was glad Max wasn't there to hear that. He might have had something to say on the subject. She glanced at Stevie, and Stevie glanced at her. The joke was shared with the glance.

Kate and her father met the carload of Hansons and Lakes at the small terminal that served private airplanes. It took a while to sort out bags and stow them on the plane that would take them Westward. It took even longer to hug and say good-bye and for the parents to remind the girls that they were supposed to be good and helpful and to ride carefully.

"If she tells me to brush my teeth every night, I'm going to growl," Stevie whispered to Carole.

"Don't bother. She will. My father already did."

Stevie's mother came over for one final hug. "Michael just told me he might actually miss you," she said. Stevie smiled. That was a pretty big compliment from the person she usually referred to as her "bratty younger brother." She gave Michael a final hug.

"Don't forget to brush your teeth," he whispered. She knew then that he'd overheard her remark to Carole. She did the only logical thing. She growled in his ear. But she also gave him an extra hug, too. Maybe she would miss him as well.

Finally, the last bag was stowed, the last seat taken, the last seat belt fastened. They were off.

Although it was a long flight, the girls thoroughly enjoyed themselves. Since Frank Devine was busy at the controls, it gave the girls an unlimited opportunity to have a Saddle Club meeting. Although Kate lived far away and they only got to see her occasionally, she was officially an out-of-town member of The Saddle Club. She was as horse crazy as they were.

Thousands of feet above the Allegheny Mountains, they talked about Pine Hollow. Crossing the Mississippi, the subject was Starlight's training. Over the plains states, talk turned to the Bar None, the Devines' dude ranch. Stevie wanted an update on her favorite horse, Stewball. Kate assured her that Stewball was as ornery, stubborn, and brilliant as ever. He was the best cow horse Stevie had ever seen and could cut cattle out of a bunch or round up a maverick without much help at all from his rider. As they neared the Rockies, Stevie and Carole asked Kate more about High Meadow. It turned out she didn't have much more information than they did. She did tell them that there would be fifteen campers besides themselves and that they would be running the ranch like a working ranch. This wasn't a glamorous camp or dude ranch. It was fashioned after the self-sufficient farms and cattle ranches that existed in the West when it was first settled.

"We'll be growing our own food, animal and vegetable. It's a serious work camp," Kate said.

"Sounds like serious fun to me," Stevie said.

"Me, too," Carole agreed. "But does 'self-sufficient' mean like no running water?"

"Of course not," Kate said. "It's a modern setup. Water *and* electricity. Heat, too, though I think we'll want to use the big stone fireplace, which Eli told me about, on those cool summer nights in the Rockies."

That did it for Stevie. She couldn't wait. It was just too exciting, and she knew it was going to be wonderful. She'd have all these wonderful new experiences, *and* she'd have the outstanding opportunity to tell some kids what to do and have them do it. It was going to be the greatest summer of her life.

"I can't wait," Carole said, as if she'd been reading or at least sharing Stevie's thoughts.

"Well, fortunately, you won't have to," said Frank from the pilot's seat. "Because we're just about there."

The girls looked out the window and saw what appeared to be a wall of mountains in the distance. They were jagged and craggy and snowcapped and simply spectacular. They seemed to the girls to be an invitation to adventure.

The plane descended smoothly, and within a few minutes they had landed. Jeannie was there to greet them. She invited Frank to drive with them to High Meadow, but when she said it was just a two-hour drive, he said he thought he'd better get on back to the Bar None. He'd only stay on the ground long enough to grab a bite to eat and refuel. He helped load the duffel bags into the pickup truck, gave Kate a hug, and whispered some final admonitions in her ear, and they were off. Later Kate admitted that he'd told her to be good and to brush her teeth every night.

"Parents," Stevie said with a sigh that conveyed a great deal to all of the girls.

"They're supposed to say that kind of thing," Jeannie said, defending the older generation. "Otherwise you wouldn't know for sure they were parents."

"Right," Stevie said. "But I promise you when I get to be a parent, I'll *never* say that kind of thing. At least not in public. And besides, what is this? Now that you're an old married lady, you're turning into a parent-type?"

Jeannie smiled. "I don't think so," she said. "It's just that now that Eli and I have fifteen young kids in our care, it makes you more aware of responsibilities."

Carole could tell that she meant it. That made her

all the happier that she and her friend were there to help.

"Don't worry, Jeannie," Carole said. "The Saddle Club is here to help, and when we put our minds to it, we can do anything."

"Definitely," Stevie added. "For instance, I don't think Eli ever would have noticed you and you guys never would have gotten married if it weren't for us, right?"

Jeannie glanced at her. "Don't take away all of my illusions," she said. "I like to think I had something to do with it."

"Sure, go ahead," Stevie allowed. "But I think we had something to do with it, too."

Jeannie agreed because she knew it was true, but she made them promise not to tell Eli. He had never known their part in getting the two of them together. They agreed to keep the secret.

The talk turned then to High Meadow as the girls pumped Jeannie about what they'd be doing. Everything sounded wonderful to the girls, but Jeannie kept saying how much work it was. The third time she used the word responsibility, Stevie got a little concerned.

"What's the big deal here?" she asked. "It's just a camp, right?"

"I wouldn't say 'just' if I were you," Jeannie said. "It's a lot of work."

"Well, that's what we're here for," Carole reminded Stevie as well as herself.

Jeannie looked at her passengers and smiled. "Yes, and I'm glad you are. You'll find this quite a challenge."

"I love challenges," Stevie said. "Especially when they have to do with horses. Look, between us, we've got probably more than thirty years of riding and horse care experience. We can do anything you need us to do. And I've got a lot of experience working with younger kids, like my brother Michael, so that part will be a breeze."

"And I know how to organize groups," Carole said. "I haven't lived with a Marine Corps colonel all these years without picking up a thing or two."

"Ditto on that for me," Kate said. "Plus, I know a lot about ranching from the Bar None."

"Looks to me like your troubles are over," Stevie said.

"Looks to *me* like yours have just begun!" Jeannie countered. But even in the fading daylight, the girls could tell she was smiling. They knew they'd made her feel better, and that made them feel better, too.

Finally, as the last of the sun dropped behind the mountains, the truck turned into the long twisting drive of High Meadow. Jeannie drove them straight to their bunkhouse, a small cabin with two sets of bunk beds, shelves for clothes, a modest but working bathroom, and a small potbellied stove. It looked a lot like the cabin they stayed in at the Bar None, and that made it feel like home.

"It's getting late now," Jeannie said. "We pretty much live by the sun here, so you might as well just unpack and go to bed. Eli left a snack for you if you're hungry. We'll see you in the morning, okay?"

"Okay," the girls agreed.

Jeannie smiled. "All the campers can't wait to meet you. They've heard so much about you." With that she pulled the door closed and left them.

Stevie couldn't help feeling a bit smug as she emptied her overloaded duffel. The campers probably would be impressed with how much the three of them knew about horses.

The snack turned out to be graham crackers and milk. The girls were hungry for it, and it tasted good. Normally, the three of them would have found lots of things to talk about, but a long day of doing nothing but traveling and talking had made them very tired. The lights were out in the main house and in the nearby bunkhouses, which the girls presumed held the fifteen campers. Very quickly, they pulled on their pajamas and climbed into their own beds. Kate switched the lights off.

Tired as she was, Stevie couldn't sleep. She lay in bed, acutely aware of the darkness. At home there were streetlights and even the glow of the city and its surrounding suburbs that seemed to fill the night sky. Here in the mountains, hours from the nearest city— even from the nearest town—there was no urban glow, no streetlights. Just stars and the moon.

After a while, Stevie's eyes became accustomed to the darkness, and she found she could see around the bunkhouse. There was plenty of room, since the bunkhouse was meant for four, not three. Stevie liked the cheerful roundness of the potbellied stove. It felt welcoming, even when not lit. She could see the bunk above her, where Carole was sleeping soundly, and from across the room she could hear Kate's gentle breathing in the top bunk. Beneath that was the empty bed, the one that by all rights belonged to Lisa.

With that thought, Stevie fell asleep.

5

Dear Stevie and Carole,

Bonjour. *That's what they say here a lot. It means hello or good day. They also say* merci *and then they say a million other things that I don't have a chance of understanding. It's really difficult. I know I've been studying French at school, but what you need in school and what you need in Paris are two very different things.*

My parents are crazy about being here in Paris, but they are worse in the language than I am and sometimes it leads to trouble. For example, today Dad thought he was getting lamb for lunch, but ended up with a tongue sandwich. Ugh. He won't make that mistake again.

We've been to the Eiffel Tower and the Louvre and we've traveled everywhere on the Metro, which is what they call the subway. In fact, we've done more traveling on the Metro than we planned since Mom got confused about which train we were supposed to take. None of us likes being lost!

Lisa tapped her pen on the paper, trying to think how she could tell her friends about her trip. Some of the things she was doing were interesting, and she wanted them to know that. Some of the things were difficult. She was having a lot of trouble with the language. She wasn't used to being in a place where it was hard to say what she wanted or needed. She'd tried to talk to her parents about it, but it was as if they didn't want to admit it was a problem. They seemed too afraid that, maybe, they weren't having as good a time as they thought they'd paid for. As a result, her father had eaten every bit of his tongue sandwich, and hadn't grimaced once. That struck Lisa as a little phony, but she also recognized that it was her parents, and not she, who were doing the paying. She felt she needed to share some of her fears, and some of her victories, with someone who would understand. That could only be Stevie and Carole—her two best friends who seemed to understand everything. She missed them terribly, and that was definitely the hardest part of all about being in Europe. But she couldn't tell them that. If she did, they might be worried about her, and if they were worried about her, it could ruin their summer. Lisa tapped her pen some more and then began writing again.

We also went to a museum in something that used to be a train station, the Musée d'Orsay. I really liked that place. They have a very pretty collection of paintings there by Impressionists. I wouldn't mind going back there. I didn't like the Louvre too much. It was crammed with people and Mom kept running up to guards to ask them where we could find the "Mona Lisa." They all looked at her blankly. It turns out that the French call that painting "La Joconde." See what I mean about confusing?

Actually, sometimes it's fun not to know what to say. After we'd walked our feet off, Mom wanted to walk some more. I wanted to take a nap. They finally agreed to let me stay in the hotel room by myself for an hour. The place is overbooked, so I'm on a rollaway bed in my parents' room, which is okay except for the fact that when I took the bed out of the closet, I could tell it had a broken wheel and that meant that it had this humungous bump in the center of it. No way I could sleep on it. I know I could have taken a nap on Mom's bed, but I decided to see if I could handle the problem myself.

I went down to the hotel desk and there was this cute bellboy who didn't speak a word of English. I pulled out my phrase book, but there wasn't anything even close to "The wheel on my rollaway bed is broken."

I smiled nicely, took a deep breath, and did my best. I said, "Le pneu sur mon lit est cassé." Roughly translated, it means "The tire on top of my bed is broken." At first the guy just looked at me blankly. Then he burst into laughter. It sounds awful, but he wasn't laughing at me, really. He was just laughing because what I'd said was so funny. And then the most wonderful thing happened. He actually understood me. He told me attendez, which I knew meant I was supposed to wait, and he brought me a new bed without a broken wheel.

Maybe this place isn't so confusing after all. I just hope I don't order a tongue sandwich by mistake the way Dad did!

I've been thinking about you a lot because I haven't seen a horse since we got here. I wish I could talk to you or get letters from you. I can't wait to read your diaries and learn everything that's happening.

Send lots of love to Kate, Eli, and Jeannie. Tell all the campers everything you've ever taught me about riding and they'll do fine.

Love,

Lisa

* * *

Dear Diary (or really Lisa since that's who's going to read this eventually. I certainly don't plan on looking at it again!)

I can't believe the day we just had! Both Stevie and Kate are sleeping soundly, but I have a lot on my mind and I can't sleep.

The day started off wrong, and it just never got any better. First of all, we were so tired that when the bell rang to wake us up, we just fell right back asleep again. Yesterday, all that traveling was more tiring than any of us had realized. So, when the breakfast bell rang, we did the same thing. Eventually, Jeannie came and woke us up. She was more or less nice about it, but we're here to help, not to cause trouble. We were causing trouble then because there was going to be a ride and nobody could go until we were ready.

It didn't get much better when we went for our ride. I guess Eli and Jeannie must have been talking about us to the campers who have been here a

45

couple of days already. They took one look at Stevie and me in our brand new Western riding clothes and they started calling us dudes. Most of them are from out West and they don't have a very high opinion of English riding. They've got a lot to learn on that subject, but we didn't do much of a job teaching them today.

First of all, I was having trouble with my horse. He's a good horse (I don't think there's any such thing as a bad horse, just bad riders), but we aren't used to one another yet. I forgot for one little second that in Western riding you use neck reining. The horse didn't do what I wanted and three of the kids kept laughing about it. Little monsters. Remind me to tell you more about Lois, Larry, and Linc. Stevie dubbed them the L-ions. It's just like her to come up with something like that. Anyway, these kids are really obnoxious, and I'm sure they're going to be our biggest problem.

Check that. I'm not sure they're going to be our biggest problem. I'm beginning to think that we are going to be our biggest problems. We don't seem to have any idea of what's going on. Every time the triangle rang, everybody else knew exactly what to do and Stevie, Kate, and I were left standing there, looking blankly at one another. The kids thought it was hysterical. Eli seemed a little perturbed and Jeannie, who never quite recovered from having to dig us out of bed this morning, just looked peeved.

What's weird is that the three of us arrived here thinking of ourselves as Eli and Jeannie's saviors. We thought they had all these gigantic problems that we were going to solve and now it looks like the three of us—Stevie and me particularly—are just causing more problems.

And I haven't even told you what happened when we tried to help in the garden this afternoon. Trust me, you don't want to know. I'll only say that it had to do with a worm that one of the L-ions dug up and everybody else thought it was a riot. It wasn't.

So, although Dad always tells me not to complain, here I am complaining. I can't help it. If we don't start being useful to Eli and Jeannie pretty soon, I'm sure they're going to want to put us on a plane and send us back home. I wouldn't blame them one bit, either.

But I'm not going to let that happen. Neither will Stevie or Kate. We came here to be helpful and we're going to be helpful. Whatever it is that Eli and Jeannie need us to do, we'll do. If we don't know what we're supposed to do, we'll ask, and we'll learn, really fast. At least I hope so.

Eli told us what our morning chores are for

tomorrow. Stevie's going to work in the vegetable patch (no worms!) and I'm supposed to collect eggs from the henhouse. Kate is going to help with the kitchen crew.

So, when do we get to ride again? Ooops, that sounded like a complaint. I didn't mean it. I may even cross it out. No I won't. This is a diary and diaries are supposed to be honest. Grrr.

Good night.
                    Carole

Carole put down her pen and closed the book. She hardly had time to turn out the light before she was asleep.

"How do you know which weed is always going to be a weed and which is going to be an onion?" Stevie asked Eli.

"The onions are the light green straight shoots," Eli said patiently. "Everything else is a weed."

"Including her," Linc hissed to Lois, obviously intending to be overheard by Stevie.

Stevie grimaced. She didn't like not knowing what she was doing, especially when she'd been invited to High Meadow because of what she supposedly knew. Linc and his friends, Lois and Larry, clearly thought the Saddle Club girls were totally idiotic dudes, and Stevie had to admit that so far she and her friends hadn't been able to do anything that might change their minds.

Stevie knew how to handle brats. After all, she was the sister of three of them. Her mind raced for a quick comeback, something to do with her various torture techniques, but she bit her tongue. She and her friends had come here to be peacemakers, not trouble-makers. It wouldn't help Eli and Jeannie at all if she got into a horrendous fight, tempting though it might be.

"I've just never weeded a garden before," she said nicely to Linc. "See, I live in a suburb and the only farms around are horse farms. I know a lot about horses, but I don't know much about farms. I'll make a deal with you, though. I'll teach you everything I know about horses if you'll help me with the farming. Okay?"

"No thanks," Linc said. "I don't want to learn any-thing about that sissy kind of riding you do."

"What do you know about English riding?" Stevie asked, as nicely as she could. She really wanted to throttle the little brat, but Eli was watching and she thought it would be a bad move in front of the boss on her second day on the job.

"I know I don't want to do it."

"Me, neither," Lois piped in. "Give me a real horse with a real saddle who does real work and I'm happy. I don't need to train a horse to dance to music or jump some phony fence, pretending to chase after a fox."

There were a thousand things Stevie could have

said. The first five hundred were put-downs and the next five hundred had to do with Lois and Linc's gross misunderstanding of what English riding was all about. But instinct told Stevie that none of them would have done any good and almost certainly would have done harm. Instead, she did the one thing Stevie almost never did: She didn't say anything.

She just yanked weeds. Really hard.

Things seemed to be going a little better for Kate in the kitchen. She and Jeannie were doing the cleanup work after breakfast. Three of the campers were supposed to be helping them by wiping off the tables in the dining room. The last time Kate had looked into the dining room, though, they were actually sitting at one of the tables, playing. They were pretending the salt and pepper shakers were cattle and they were on a roundup. At least they were playing quietly.

Kate considered her options. The first option, of course, was to go remind the kids what they were supposed to do. This was a ranch, and everybody had chores to do. They were no different.

Then she saw the way one of the kids, Larry, was looking at her. One glance and she knew he was trouble. The look said he'd do whatever she asked him to do and he'd do it so badly that she'd have to redo it herself. Since she was well convinced she'd end up doing the work anyway, she decided not to make an issue of it. While they rounded up salt and pepper shakers, she wiped tables. She did it quickly and well. It only took a few minutes. When she returned to the kitchen, Jeannie asked her how the kids were doing with the table wiping. Kate explained what had happened.

"You shouldn't have done it," Jeannie said. "It's their job; they can do it."

"But they would have done it all wrong, just to spite me," Kate said. "I know."

"Then they would have done it again until they did it right," Jeannie said. "They're supposed to learn to carry their own weight on a working ranch. What you did teaches them that they can get away without carrying anything."

"Oh," Kate said, knowing full well that Jeannie was right and feeling as though she'd just let everybody down. She was in the middle of figuring out how she could make it right—make Larry and the other kids do an extra chore just to stress Jeannie's point about everybody carrying his or her own weight—when a shriek came from the henhouse. Jeannie dropped the pot she was scrubbing, Kate flung down the dish towel, and the three kids in the dining room abandoned the salt-and-pepper roundup game to see what was going on.

What they found was Carole, holding her wrist and obviously trying to hold back some tears. She was the one who had screamed. Kate and Stevie ran over to her and asked her what had happened.

"She bit me!" Carole yelled loudly.

The first thought that entered Stevie's head was that Carole meant that Lois had bitten her, though Stevie knew perfectly well that Lois had been with her in the onion patch. Then she realized Carole meant she'd been bitten by a hen.

Carole held out her wrist for her friends to inspect. It was swollen and bruised. The skin was broken, and there was a small bead of blood.

"She hurt you that badly over one measly egg?" Stevie asked.

"Oh, they can get pretty feisty sometimes," Eli said. Carole could have sworn there was a little smirk in his tone—as if he'd known it and hadn't realized he'd have to tell an Eastern dude something so simple and so obvious.

"At least I got the egg," Carole said, holding it up triumphantly for everyone to see. What they saw was a fresh egg with a big crack in it. "It should be okay if we eat it today or tomorrow."

"And scramble it," Larry whispered loudly. Lois and Linc laughed. So did four or five other kids who were standing nearby. It didn't make Carole feel any better.

"Are there any bandages around?" Carole asked.

"Sure," Eli said. "They're in the bathroom in the main house. Help yourself."

53

The look on Carole's face told her friends that right then she was incapable of helping herself. Both Stevie and Kate volunteered to go with her. They looked to Eli for permission. "I guess so," he said. "But hurry back, we're going for a ride soon."

Carole handed the egg to Eli, and she and her friends headed indoors. The last thing they heard before they stepped up onto the farmhouse porch was one of the L-ions asking the other two: "How many English riders does it take to put on a Band-Aid?"

The girls didn't wait to hear the answer. They simply fled to the bathroom.

"This isn't going well, is it?" Kate asked, putting words to the question that was on all of their minds.

"Not as far as I can tell," said Stevie. "And from the look of this cut, Carole and the hen would agree with that."

"I feel so stupid," Carole said, looking more closely at the cut. "I just never thought the hen might not like it."

"You had no way of knowing," Kate reminded her. "You've never collected eggs before."

"I've read about it in books. I've seen it in movies. The way they show it, it's always the kid in the family who does it. I sort of thought that meant it wasn't hard or dangerous. I guess I was wrong. I just feel stupid."

"Me, too," Stevie said. When Kate and Carole

looked at her questioningly, she explained about not knowing the difference between an onion and a weed. Kate then told her friends about the kids who'd wangled her into doing their job.

"I don't think we're quite the stars here that we were hoping to be," Stevie said.

"And I don't think we've fooled anybody," said Kate. "The kids all seemed to have this gigantic expectation about how wonderful we were and look at what we've done."

"Yeah," Carole agreed. "I got the impression that Eli and Jeannie have spent the last couple of days telling the campers we're geniuses. We've let them down, too."

"Cheer up, guys," Kate said, finding a bright side of the situation. "Eli and Jeannie certainly never told anybody that we were geniuses at weeding gardens, wiping tables, or collecting eggs, did they? They told them we were geniuses at horseback riding and that's what we're about to do. It's the perfect chance for us to redeem ourselves."

Stevie and Carole were quiet for a minute. That was partly because Stevie was trying to choose the best way to put the bandage on Carole's cut. It was also because they were considering Kate's observation.

"Think so?" Stevie said after a while.

"Definitely," Kate said.

Stevie decided Kate's certainty was good enough for

her. There were definitely better times ahead. Carole believed it, too. Stevie admired her handiwork on Carole's wrist, crumpled the bandage wrapper, dropped it in the wastebasket, and said, "Let's go riding!"

The girls met up with the campers and Eli at the large paddock where Eli was showing them how to cut out the horses they wanted to ride for the day. It was a job that Kate had watched Eli do a hundred times at the Bar None, and she knew how to do it almost as well as he did. Obviously Eli had been expecting her to help with this job because he'd already saddled up her horse.

She hopped over the fence and mounted up. Eli gave her a welcoming smile. Eli hadn't ever been much of a talker. A smile from him said more than a thousand words. It gave Kate the confidence she'd been lacking ever since she'd blown it on cleanup duty earlier.

"I'll work on the left side," she suggested. Eli nodded. Kate went to work.

Eli was cutting about twenty horses. The herd was more than fifty, and the routine at High Meadow seemed to be about what it had been at Bar None. Each day they'd take some of the horses out for use that day. Others would get a day of rest. Eli certainly knew the herd. It had always been part of his job at the Bar None to judge which horses would be good for which riders. As he chose the horses to cut out of the pack, Kate just made it her job to see to it that that horse stayed cut out. The two of them had the help of Eli's dog, Mel, a caramel-colored mixed breed and the smartest working dog Kate had ever seen.

When the day's twenty horses were clear of the herd, Eli and Mel brought them over toward the campers and began assigning each child to one horse. Kate guarded the rest of the herd, so that they stayed away from the day's horses. She looked around for the best way to do that. There was a gate in the fence behind her. It opened into a smaller paddock where a lone horse grazed, apparently oblivious to all the activity around. The easiest way to keep the horses separate would be to herd them all into the smaller paddock, at least for the time being while the day's horses were being saddled. She lifted the latch on the high gate, swung it open, and began to shoo the horses into the smaller paddock.

It took her only a few minutes. She rode back to where Eli, Carole, and Stevie were helping the young riders put the saddles on their assigned horses. Everything looked just the way it should. It felt good to Kate to know that, finally, she and her friends were being helpful.

"I put the rest of the herd into that smaller field," she reported to Eli, who looked up from his work to see what she was talking about.

"Can't do that," he said.

"I just did," she said. "Why not?"

"That there is Arthur," he said, pointing to the horse who'd been in the field by himself. "He belongs to the man who owns this farm. Man's devoted to the creature, though I don't know why. Every time Arthur gets in with other horses, he's trouble. Got to get the rest of the herd out."

"Can't I just take Arthur out?"

"Nope."

Kate sighed. Getting thirty horses into a paddock with one other horse was easy. Getting thirty horses out of a paddock, leaving just one, wasn't easy. She was annoyed with herself. She should have asked Eli where to keep the rest of the herd. She had made the mistake, and now she had to correct it.

It took Kate a while to get the herd rounded up and out of the paddock. There were plenty of fenced areas around the farm so figuring out where to put them wasn't hard. Keeping Arthur in and getting the herd out proved to be more difficult, but she did it. By the time she finished, all the campers were in their saddles and waiting for her. She didn't enjoy riding back to the group as they sat there, watching. It felt very humiliating. She decided to rise above it.

"Let's go for a ride!" she said brightly. Eli clicked his tongue and nudged his horse. The ride began.

* * *

58

THAT NIGHT, WHEN Eli announced a camp-fire cowboy sing, Kate, Carole, and Stevie begged off, saying they were still tired from their plane trip. Nobody believed them, but nobody stopped them either. The girls figured the campers were glad to be rid of them. They didn't know what Eli and Jeannie thought. They weren't sure they cared.

"Last one into her pajamas is a rotten egg," Stevie declared. She was already in her pajamas by then so she had an unfair advantage. While Carole and Kate followed suit, she made use of the time by building a little fire in their potbellied stove. They weren't going to sing cowboy songs, but Stevie thought there was a good chance they would sing the blues.

Once in her pajamas, Carole flopped into one of the folding chairs and watched the flames flicker to life in the stove.

"At first, I thought the low point of the day was when the hen bit me," she said. "But then it actually came when I fell off the horse." There was a moment of quiet, and then she repeated the words as if to be sure they were true: "I . . . fell . . . off . . . the . . . horse." It didn't sound any more real the second time, but it was just as true.

During the trail ride, Eli had asked Carole to bring up the rear. That was a compliment. In general on trail rides, the best rider was in the front and the second best in the back. There had to be a strong rider at the rear to be sure everybody was safe and to be in charge if something happened. Considering her track record since she'd arrived, Carole was pleased that Eli had asked her to take that position. Apparently, he didn't hold an angry hen against her.

Being in the saddle and on a trail ride had seemed like exactly the right thing to heal all the humiliation of the previous events. Carole had often felt that being with horses made everything else better. She'd been content. She'd not only been riding, but she'd also been able to talk about it. One of the campers—not one of the L-ions—had asked her about the differences between English and Western riding, and it was an opportunity to explain something. She loved explaining things. Her friends sometimes teased her that she gave twenty-five-cent answers to nickel questions, but Carole was, nevertheless, happy as she shared her knowledge with the younger rider.

Then the trail had begun leading upwards. Eli had passed the word back to remind all the riders to lean forward, compensating for the change in balance as the trail got steeper. Carole, however, was so involved in her explanation that she wasn't paying attention. She didn't lean forward far enough, and the next thing she knew, she'd slid right out of the saddle and onto the rocky trail. She'd felt like a total idiot. Her horse stopped patiently, as if he'd had plenty of experience waiting for dumb dudes, and she'd gotten right back into the saddle, but not before everybody had noticed, and most people had laughed—especially the L-ions.

Eli had then suggested that Kate take up the rear, saying he wanted to be sure Carole hadn't hurt herself. He was obviously just being nice about the fact that he couldn't trust her at the rear anymore.

"Carole, it could have happened to anyone," Stevie said.

"Sure, it could have. I fell off a horse once," Kate added.

"Right. When you were about eight years old," Carole said numbly.

"At least you didn't put thirty horses in the wrong paddock," Kate said, remembering her own worst moment.

"Or be laughed at for not knowing an onion for a weed," Stevie chimed in.

All in all, it had not been a wonderful day.

There was a knock at the door. The girls turned, wondering who on earth would want to be anywhere near them. It was Jeannie.

"Can I come in? I don't think I can stand another verse of 'Home on the Range.' It makes me think of that stove. . . ."

She was making a joke about all the cooking she'd been doing. The very idea of making a joke after the dreadful day they'd had seemed totally weird.

"Are you okay?" Stevie asked.

"More or less," Jeannie said. "I haven't had a minute to talk to you girls and tell how glad we are you're here."

"You are?"

"We sure are," she said. "See, we've had a problem with the staff. Four campers dropped out at the last minute and never paid us anything. We had two counselors signed up, but we had to let them go because we didn't have enough income. We're really relying on you three for a lot and asking you to do an awful lot of work for us. I just wanted to let you know that it's going to be tough."

"I guess we know that and we don't mind," Kate said. "I've seen how hard my parents have had to work to keep the Bar None going. I also know how much you and Eli helped them. I want to be of some use to you guys with High Meadow."

"Me, too," Stevie said. Carole nodded agreement.

"Well, thanks," Jeannie said. "I guess I'd better get back to my home on the range—the stove, I mean. I've got to figure out what I'm going to make for breakfast. See you," she said, and she was gone.

"We're letting them down," Stevie said. "That was a pep talk, wasn't it?"

"Sounded like it to me," Kate agreed.

"We can help. We really can," Carole said. "We

just have to figure out how and to stop doing stupid things, like falling off horses."

"We just have to try harder," Stevie agreed.

They all knew that was true, but so far their trying hadn't done much good. How much harder could they try? And how much good would it do?

WHEN THE TRIANGLE rang the next morning, three sleepy Saddle Club girls rolled out of bed and into their clothes as quickly as they could. They wanted to do everything possible to be helpful and make Eli and Jeannie's load easier.

Ten minutes later they filed into the dining room, ready for a new day.

Once breakfast had been served to all the campers, the girls each took a plate of flapjacks and sausages and sat down at the long table with the kids. It was tempting for them to eat by themselves at a smaller table, but they'd never get to know the campers well unless they spent time with them, and they'd never be useful as counselors unless they knew the kids. They did try very hard to avoid sitting with the L-ions, though that was difficult with three of them and only fifteen campers.

Carole wondered where Eli and Jeannie were. Maybe she should be in the kitchen helping out. Then she noticed that the light on the extension phone was lit in the dining room. Eli was obviously talking to someone. Carole didn't think she could help with that, so she ate her breakfast.

A few minutes later, Eli entered the dining room. There was a happy look on his face—a happier look than Carole and her friends had seen since they'd arrived at High Meadow. Something was up and it just had to be good.

He cleared his throat. "I've got some news," he began. It turned out that he'd been talking with his neighbor on the telephone. The man had a herd of cattle that needed to be moved from one grazing area to another about fifty miles away. There were a lot of cattle and the man was shorthanded. He'd called to see if Eli had anybody around who could do some cowpunching for him.

"So, do I?" Eli asked.

The campers all looked at one another. "You mean us?" one of the kids asked.

"I think so," Eli said. "The fact is, I was going to borrow some of his cattle to have a sort of make-believe cattle drive, but this is much better. You all can have some experience with the real thing, and we can do my neighbor a favor at the same time."

And High Meadow can get paid for helping with the drive, Stevie thought to herself. Maybe that was the best news of all. Some people thought Stevie didn't know much about money since she never seemed to have any. She always spent her allowance as fast as she got it. The fact was that because she was always out of it, she was very sensitive to what it was like for other people to be out of it. It wasn't a nice feeling. And since Eli had lost those four campers at the last minute, he must be terribly worried about money—just the way Stevie would be if her parents suddenly cut her allowance. Maybe they wouldn't make a lot for doing this, but it would be something, and something was better than nothing.

"*Ya-hooooo!*" Stevie called out enthusiastically. One thing about Stevie was that her enthusiasm was always contagious. When she was excited about something, everybody around her always was, too. Now almost all the campers raised their hands when Eli asked who wanted to go along on the cattle drive.

Carole watched this and was as excited as everybody else about the trip. She'd gone on a two-day cattle drive on her first visit to the Bar None, and it had been an unforgettable experience. She'd hoped they'd be doing more of it this summer.

It turned out that three campers—Linc of the

L-ions and two others—didn't want to go on the drive. One of the other two, a boy named Ellis, had a pretty bad cold and needed to stay around the ranch. The other one, Jack, just didn't like the idea of sleeping under the stars for all those nights.

Jeannie would stay at the ranch with the kids. There was a lot of work to be done no matter how many people were there, so somebody had to stay. The garden had to be weeded, the animals tended, and generally the place had to be kept up. These thoughts flashed through Carole's mind. What also flashed through at the same time was that there was a lot of work for *any* one person to do. And the final thought that came to her was that she and her friends were at High Meadow to be as helpful as possible. Eli, Stevie, and Kate were more than capable of looking after a herd of cattle and twelve campers, especially when the campers would be too busy riding the herd to get into trouble. Carole wasn't needed on the roundup. She was needed at the ranch.

"I'll stay here," she said. Stevie and Kate looked at her in surprise. Stevie's look was almost one of alarm.

"Jeannie needs me," she said simply.

"I'll stay, too," Stevie said.

"No way," said Carole. "Eli needs you."

It was true, and Carole knew that that was the right way to do it. If it meant that she wouldn't get to do anywhere near as much riding as she wanted for a couple of days, what difference would it make? She was doing what was right, and that felt good.

"Fine," Eli said, confirming who was leaving and who was staying. "I want you all to go pack your bed-rolls, a change of clothes, and your most necessary personal items. We will leave right after morning chores."

"Can't we skip the morning chores?" Lois asked.

Eli gave her a withering look. Stevie found herself a little relieved to know that Eli found at least this one of the L-ions as unpleasant to deal with as she did.

Carole finished her last pancake and began gathering the plates to start work in the kitchen. There were a lot of sandwiches to make for the first meal the cowpokes would eat on the trail. After that the rancher would supply meals from a chuck wagon. In the olden days, a chuck wagon was a horse-drawn covered wagon that rode with the herd. In more modern times, it was a pickup truck complete with a stove and a refrigerator. The chuck wagon would meet them at the first night's campsite.

Carole and Jeannie worked together in the kitchen, quickly and efficiently. First, they cleaned up after breakfast. Carole had the job of seeing to it that the campers cleaned up the dining room well. She found that when she told them they couldn't go on the cattle drive until after the job was done, well, they worked twice as hard!

Once the campers got busy packing their bedrolls, Carole and Jeannie began making lunch: sandwiches, fruit, dessert, and drinks. They set up an assembly line and got the job done very quickly.

As they worked, Carole was too busy to think about the trip her friends would be taking, but when they passed out the lunch bags and looked at the gear all packed and rolled and tied to the back of each saddle, it occurred to Carole that the trip Kate and Stevie were going on was a very far cry from the two-day cattle drive they'd done on the Bar None. They'd hardly left the Devines' property for that one. Now a group of kids, two young counselors, and one real cowboy were taking a very large herd a long distance. They'd be gone for the better part of a week.

As she thought about this, Carole was surprised that she wasn't more envious. But Kate and Stevie were doing something they needed to do, helping Eli, being counselors. And she was being helpful in another way, staying with Jeannie, looking after the three campers who'd be there, too. She was being responsible. That, alone, was enough to make her feel happy about her decision.

"Okay, what's my first job?" Carole asked, turning to Jeannie.

Jeannie scrunched her eyebrows in thought, and then she spoke. "Well, since you're giving up a horseback trip, I think you have the right to have your first job be a horse job. Saddle up a pony for yourself and round up all the horses, except Arthur of course, and put them in the field on the far side of the barn. Get the campers to help you with that. They should be on ponies, too. Then you can set your own ponies out in the field as well."

"Yes, ma'am," Carole said, saluting sharply just the way her father had taught her. Rounding up horses wasn't exactly the same as rounding up a herd of cattle, but it was certainly something she could do. She also liked the idea of showing the campers how to do it. She truly felt she was being helpful to Eli and Jeannie, once again confirming that she'd made the right decision.

"HENRY THE SECOND built the round tower, you know,"
Mrs. Atwood said.

"Imagine that!" Lisa uttered. She was trying to
sound excited, but she wasn't feeling it. Her father
didn't seem particularly excited either and wasn't
even making a pretense of it. He just kept looking
around at the shops in the town of Windsor.

"Isn't there one of those pubs around here some
place?" he asked.

"Later, dear, later. It's only ten-thirty now and we
have so much to see before lunch."

"Everything except the castle," Lisa said. They'd
taken the train from London to Windsor, about an
hour's ride, expecting to be able to have the tour of
the castle, but it turned out that the queen was in

residence now, so they couldn't visit it. Mr. Atwood had remarked to Mrs. Atwood that perhaps she should have checked where the queen was staying before they got onto a train. Mrs. Atwood had said it didn't matter at all that they couldn't get into the castle proper. The town of Windsor itself was positively filled with memorable sights.

"Perhaps we'll see the queen driving through the town in a limousine," Mrs. Atwood said cheerfully.

Mr. Atwood looked at her. "Think that means she might spot us as a nice group of American tourists and invite us in for a cup of tea?" he asked sarcastically.

Mrs. Atwood stopped talking for a few minutes.

Lisa sighed. This was frustrating. There were parts of the trip she was enjoying, but at times like these, she couldn't keep her mind on the quaint cobble-stoned streets of the town. All she could think of was the wide-open spaces of Wyoming and how much she wished she were there with her friends, riding in the Rockies, rounding up cattle, eating stew by a camp fire, singing cowboy songs, enjoying the fresh mountain air, and smelling the wildflowers and the warm, wonderful scent of horses.

"And if we go along this street for a way, we'll find the park," Mrs. Atwood said. "Park" seemed about as close as she was going to get to wide-open spaces. She followed her mother dutifully.

One thing she'd discovered about the British people was that they had nice parks. London had many really pretty ones, all of which were planted with colorful flower beds. It seemed that in the United States, flower beds in parks had to be protected with concertina wire. Here in England everybody just enjoyed the flowers without picking them. It was terribly civilized, and Lisa did like that. The park in Windsor was no exception. It had gently sloping hills with well-tended grass. Here and there were little flower beds, neatly planted for maximum enjoyment by people strolling by.

Mrs. Atwood was all for walking along every single inch of footpath in the park. Mr. Atwood was, by then, totally preoccupied with his empty stomach and decided to sit down and think about it. Lisa and her mother sat down with him.

While her parents discussed the choices they had for eating lunch, Lisa daydreamed about Wyoming. She remembered the great trips she'd had with her friends to the Bar None. She thought about the horses on the ranch. She could almost hear the clip-clop of their hooves on the open prairie land.

Then she realized that she definitely *could* hear the clip-clop of some horse's hooves, even if it wasn't a Bar None horse. The clips and clops were approaching at a very fast pace, and then they stopped. Lisa leapt up from the bench. If there was a horse around, she just had to see it.

She'd heard the horse stop just over the hilltop nearby, and in a few seconds she could see the horse, a sleek, bay Thoroughbred. What she couldn't see, however, was the rider. The horse was saddled up and riderless. One of the stirrups was twisted around its leathers, and it looked as though the horse had thrown his rider and run off.

Lisa knew just what to do. She had to find the rider and make sure he or she was okay. A rider could get badly hurt being thrown from a horse, and this park was big enough that it might be a while before anyone found the injured rider.

Lisa approached the horse, who appeared to be run out. He stood patiently while Lisa lifted his reins, and then he walked forward obediently while she led him. Lisa wanted to ride him. It was going to be the fastest way to get back to the rider he'd thrown, but she also wanted to make sure that he was over whatever had spooked him in the first place. He seemed very tame and willing. She brought him over to an empty park bench to use as a mounting block. In a matter of seconds, she was in the saddle and pleased to find that she didn't even have to adjust the stirrups. They were already the right length. She wasn't wearing appropriate clothing to ride this perfectly groomed and tacked horse, but riding was better and faster than walking. She gave the horse a gentle nudge and rode up to the crest of the hill to tell her parents where she was going.

Her mother started to protest, strongly. Lisa shrugged. She knew what she was doing, and it was a lot more important than deciding which historic pub to go to for lunch.

She followed the horse's trail as well as she could. Riding this elegant Thoroughbred was so wonderful that she almost didn't care if she ever found the rider. It was clear to her that this was a very valuable horse who probably had bloodlines that could be traced back as far as the round tower at Windsor Castle. Her mother could admire old stones. She preferred to admire horses. Not only was this an elegant horse, but his gaits were smooth and even. She alternated walking and trotting and found it utterly joyful to feel the wind on her face as the horse traced the bridle path back. For the first time since leaving the United States, Lisa was totally happy.

Then she spotted the thrown rider. It wasn't hard to figure out. There was a girl, about her own age, decked in a perfect riding outfit, standing on the edge of the bridle path, rubbing her elbow and looking annoyed.

Lisa pulled up to her. "I think I found something that belongs to you."

The relief on the girl's face was visible. "Thank you so much. I was just wondering where this fellow went." She peered at Lisa curiously. "American, are you?"

"Yup," Lisa confirmed. "My name's Lisa Atwood. I'm from Willow Creek, Virginia, U.S.A." She dismounted and held out her hand to shake.

"Lady Theresa," the downed rider said, taking Lisa's offered hand and shaking it vigorously.

Lady? She was no older than Lisa. How could she be a lady? Lisa wasn't sure what protocol called for, but she knew she couldn't help herself. "Lady Theresa? That's what people call you?"

Lady Theresa smiled. It was a warm and kind smile in response to what Lisa realized must have sounded like a rather rude question. Lisa liked this girl immediately.

"Not at all," Lady Theresa said. "My friends call me Tessa."

That didn't help Lisa very much. She tried again. "Am I a friend?"

Tessa shook her head, laughing. "No. You're a savior. But it's okay because saviors call me Tessa, too."

That was the moment when Lisa knew for sure that they would be friends forever. The girls began talking. Lisa learned that Tessa had been riding by herself because she had thought she was good enough to be safe. Lisa explained that it was never wise to ride alone. "It's almost as silly as swimming by yourself," she said. "That's why I always go riding with my friends."

"And where are they now?" Tessa asked. "I mean, you just rode over here by yourself!"

"It's a long story," Lisa said.

"Well, we have a long walk," Tessa said. "But why don't we do it on horseback? We can ride double, as long as you're in front. My ankle hurts a little. Why don't you get up first and then give me a hand?"

Lisa did that, once again finding a park bench for a mounting block. Then she offered Tessa a hand, and the two of them were ready to ride together.

"Where to, miss?" Lisa asked in a pretty good imitation of a Cockney accent. She was trying to mimic one of the London cab drivers and must have done a fairly good job of it because Tessa laughed.

"Royal stables, please."

Royal stables?

" 'Ow do oi get there?" Lisa asked, when she had recovered.

"Just over that hill and follow the path," Tessa said.

"Really the royal stables?" Lisa asked, unable to contain her curiosity.

"Really," Tessa said. "You see, my mother is a distant cousin to Her Majesty, and as a result I'm invited to ride the royal horses occasionally. Today was one of those occasions."

Lisa was having some trouble taking in all this. She was actually on a horse belonging to the royal family, riding double with a member of that family, albeit distantly related. At the same time as this was going on, her parents were on a nearby park bench, talking about lunch. To Lisa, it seemed like a dream. Then it occurred to Lisa that her parents were probably also worried about her.

"I think I'd better let my parents know where we're going," Lisa said, and she explained where they were.

"No problem," said Tessa. The two of them went back over the route that Lisa and the horse had taken to find Tessa in the first place.

Lisa's parents were much as she'd left them. Her mother was flipping through pages in the guide book, trying to find something else deadly dull to see before they left Windsor. Her father had stretched his legs out in front of him and was clasping his empty stomach.

"Mom, Dad, this is Tessa," Lisa said, introducing her new friend. "Tessa, my parents, Mr. and Mrs. Atwood."

"How do you do?" Tessa asked.

"Pleased, I'm sure," said Mrs. Atwood.

"Say, do you live around here? Do you know a good place for us to get lunch?" Mr. Atwood asked.

"I'm not sure," Tessa said. "Let me think."

"Tessa has hurt her ankle so I'm going to ride back with her to the royal stables. I should be back here in a little while."

"I'll have someone drive Lisa back," Tessa assured

the Atwoods. "In the meantime, however, there's a pleasant little restaurant next to the woollen shop."

"Oh, sure, I saw that one. It's good?"

"Best in town," Tessa said. "Why don't you go on over, and I'll have the driver drop Lisa off there. She'll be about an hour. I know she's going to want to see the stables, and you shouldn't have to wait."

"Did you say *royal stables?*" Mrs. Atwood asked. Clearly the words had taken a few minutes to sink in.

"Yup," Tessa said, doing as good a job of imitating an American accent as Lisa had done with the Cockney.

"See you later, Mom and Dad," Lisa interrupted. She wanted to get out of there before her mother tried to come along. Mrs. Atwood went absolutely bonkers over anything that had to do with the royal family. But before they were out of sight and earshot, Lisa saw her mother turn to her father and heard her say, "Isn't it nice that Lisa's not too old to play pretend with her friends?"

Behind her, Tessa started laughing. Lisa giggled, too. It was a nice thing to do with a new friend.

The royal stables were as wonderful as Lisa had expected, not because they belonged to the royal family but because they were stables containing horses. There were a few things that set this stable apart from any stable Lisa had ever seen. The first was that every single horse in there was clearly extremely valuable.

The other was that in the carriage house, there were a few carriages that were for state occasions and were exquisite antiques. Other than that, the royal stable was just like every other stable, down to the barn cats whose job was the same as it was at Pine Hollow: Keep the mouse population to a minimum!

Lisa would have liked to have spent the whole day at the stables. Tessa even hinted that they might try to get her a horse to ride so the two of them could go out on the trail together. But Lisa thought about her parents sitting alone in the restaurant, probably wondering what Lisa was up to, and she knew that she'd done all the riding she was going to do for the day.

She and Tessa had a great time together. Tessa introduced her to everyone in the stables as "the American who rounded up my horse and saved my life." It was more than a slight exaggeration, but it did seem to give Lisa a certain status among the groomers. They saluted her and thanked her.

Finally, it was time for her to go. The stables' driver said he'd be more than happy to drop Lisa off at the restaurant next to the woollen shop. Hastily, Lisa and Tessa scribbled their addresses on paper and exchanged them, promising to write often. Tessa even said she thought she might be coming to America for a visit soon.

"I understand there are some good stables in Virginia, aren't there?"

"The *best*," Lisa assured her. "And its name is Pine Hollow. The welcome mat will always be out for you."

The girls gave each other hugs, and then the visit, the magical time, was over. Lisa hopped into the front seat of the big comfortable car, and the driver took her into town.

Her parents were ordering dessert when Lisa arrived at the restaurant. She asked for a sandwich and began to tell her parents about her adventure. Her mother just nodded and smiled sweetly. Mrs. Atwood clearly thought Lisa was still playing pretend.

"It's for real, Mom," Lisa said. "I was actually at the queen's stables."

"It must have been very interesting," said Mrs. Atwood.

Mr. Atwood just kept scanning the dessert menu. "What's trifle, do you suppose?"

Lisa sighed. There was no way either one of them would care or believe her. The adventure was hers and hers alone, until she had a chance to write to her friends about it.

Then the door to the restaurant flew open. In walked a tall man in uniform.

"Is there a Miss Lisa Atwood here?" he asked.

Lisa's parents looked alarmed. "I'm here?" Lisa said tentatively, and raised her arm.

"Oh, good," said the man approaching their table. "Her Majesty wanted to give you her personal thanks for rescuing her cousin Lady Theresa today. Her Majesty hopes you will accept this as a small token of her appreciation."

He held out a box. Lisa accepted it and opened it while everybody in the restaurant looked on. It was a small crystal horse, nearly a perfect replica of one of the Thoroughbreds from Her Majesty's stables.

Lisa's mother was absolutely speechless. It was enough to divert her father's attention from his stomach, too.

Lisa blushed with excitement. She looked up at the equerry. "Please tell Her Majesty that I was glad to help and that she really doesn't have to give me anything."

The man looked at Lisa and winked. "She knows that," he said. Then he saluted her smartly and left the restaurant.

That was when Lisa decided that maybe this trip to Europe with her parents wasn't going to be such a bore after all!

CAROLE WAS DREAMING. It was a weird dream about rows and rows of onions that needed to be weeded and pots that needed to be washed and horses that needed to be fed and groomed. Then all of a sudden, a bell rang. In her dream she was sure it was a fire alarm—just like the one that rang in school. She knew what to do in a fire drill. You were supposed to get in a neat line and walk out of the school. She and dozens of campers—all of whom had names that started with "L"—got in line with the onions and the pots and began walking in an orderly fashion.

The bell kept ringing, insistently. It wasn't a fire drill. Carole sat up in bed and opened her eyes. The bell still rang, but it wasn't exactly a bell. It was the triangle. That was very weird because it was still pitch black outside. It wasn't morning at all. Then Carole realized that if the bell was ringing at this hour, Jeannie needed her help.

She didn't bother with clothes. She just pulled on her boots and ran to the main house.

"Carole, you've got to help!" Jeannie said breathlessly.

"What's on fire?"

"Nothing," Jeannie told her. "It's the horses. They're gone!"

Carole looked over Jeannie's shoulder to the field where she'd put all the horses earlier. There was not a horse in sight.

"Well, at least we've still got Arthur," Carole said, trying very hard to find a bright side to twenty missing horses.

Jeannie looked over at the paddock where the lone horse stood quietly. "That's not Arthur," she said. "Arthur's got a crooked blaze. That horse has a star."

Carole squinted to be sure Jeannie was right. "You mean I spent an hour this morning separating all the other horses from a horse that *isn't* Arthur?"

"I guess so," Jeannie said.

Then Carole remembered that Arthur was always supposed to stay away from the herd because he was a troublemaker. She was getting a very bad feeling about this.

"What kind of trouble does Arthur cause?" she asked.

"He makes the herd roam," Jeannie said, once again indicating the empty field. "He's just a natural leader, and when he's got some horses who will follow him, he leads them. Away. See, he'll jump a fence and everybody else follows."

"But where did he go?"

Jeannie stood on her tiptoes and looked across the darkened landscape. It wasn't easy to see because there were no lights around at all, except the stars and a sliver of a moon. Then she noticed some motion on a hilltop perhaps a mile away.

"I think they are over there," she said, pointing. Carole looked. There seemed to be a number of dark patches silhouetted against the pale grass. She agreed that it was likely those were the horses.

"I'll go get them," Carole offered quickly, "Why don't you go back to bed."

Jeannie looked exhausted, and she didn't bother to protest. "Thanks, Carole," she said. "As long as you think you can handle it. I should tell you, though, that if that is our herd of horses, we could be in some real trouble. That land belongs to a neighbor who tried very hard to stop us from running the camp here this summer. He hates kids and doesn't much like anybody else, either. Eli had to promise on a stack of Bibles that he'd never even know we were here. So, while you're busy getting the horses off his land, be sure he doesn't discover you, okay?"

"Okay," Carole said. She said it because it was the only answer she could give, but she gulped at the very idea. It wasn't easy to get twenty horses to move without letting anybody know. How was she going to do it?

She wasn't sure how, but she was sure when. It had to be right away. It was 3:30 in the morning. By 4:30, the sun would start to rise. By 5:30, it would be fully light and people around here tended to wake up with the sun. It might be possible to sneak a herd off the farmer's land in the dark; it would be impossible after dawn.

Carole ran over to her bunk and slipped her jeans on over her pajamas. Her mind raced as she buttoned her shirt. She couldn't do this alone; she couldn't do this with Jeannie. Her only other choice was to get the three campers to help her.

The three of them were sleeping in the spare bedroom in the other half of Carole's bunkhouse. Waking them up would be no problem. Motivating them could cause some difficulty.

Carole wished Stevie were there. Not only would she be invaluable in helping with the roundup, but she'd also know exactly how to get the campers to be useful. Carole had found that exposure to Stevie sometimes made her think a little bit like Stevie. She

86

knew she needed a Stevian inspiration. And one came to her.

She slipped a kerchief around her neck and over her face so she looked like a bank robber. She stepped into the campers' bunk room and turned on the light.

"Okay, you rustlers, it's time to get up and steal the herd before the owner catches us. If we do this right, we'll have all them horses miles and miles away before anybody knows they're gone!"

"Huh?"

"Rustlers?" Linc asked, sitting up in bed. He was such a troublemaker that the idea of doing something —or even pretending to do something—that was against the law sounded like a really good idea to him.

"Yup, rustlers," Carole confirmed. "There's a herd of horses, about twenty head, in a field about a mile from here. We're going to have to sneak up on them on foot—and the sneaking part shouldn't be too hard because most of them are probably asleep. We'll each carry a bridle with us, and then we'll bring them on home. All by the light of the stars and the moon. Are you guys good enough for this?"

That was exactly the right question to ask. There was nothing like a challenge to get the kids up and going. Even the boy with the cold was willing to go along. Carole said it was okay as long as he wasn't coughing (he wasn't) and if he wrapped up warmly. He promised to wear a sweater and a scarf.

The four "rustlers" were ready to leave in five minutes. They stopped off at the barn to pick up the tack and began their trek across the field.

They had to go in the dark. Flashlights might have awakened neighbors or upset the herd of horses. The horses were going to be hard enough to bring home without having them upset. Carole led the way. It wasn't easy going. The ground wasn't all that smooth and was dotted with clumps of grass that were just perfect for tripping unsuspecting "rustlers." Every time Carole stumbled, she found another route and made the campers take it. She wouldn't have minded twisting her own ankle, but she hated the idea of twisting anybody else's, even Linc's.

It was turning out that Linc was perfect for this deed. He took to it like a fish to water. He got real pleasure out of being sneaky, and got right into the part of rustler.

Soon enough they approached the herd. Most of the horses were standing quietly, sleeping as they stood. A few munched on grass. One or two looked up when the "rustlers" drew near, but none of them seemed interested in going anywhere.

The first thing Carole had to do was to find Arthur. It wasn't easy locating a bay with a straight blaze. Most of the horses were bays. Plenty of them had blazes. However, she spotted one bay with a blaze who was completely surrounded by other horses. That,

Carole decided, was charisma—the trait of a natural leader. It just had to be Arthur!

She moved the adoring fans away from around the horse and slipped a bridle onto him. It wasn't hard to do, and he didn't protest. It seemed that Arthur's only undesirable quality was his tendency to lead other horses astray. Other than that, he was a fine, obedient horse. Carole hoped so, anyway, since she was going to have to ride him bareback.

Once she had his bridle on, she gathered her "rustlers" and told them what they were to do. First of all, each of them was to pick a pony to ride, put the bridle on it, and then mount up. Carole would help them.

Linc found a dappled gray. Ellis located a sorrel, and Jack found a bay for himself. Quietly, but surely, each put the bridle on his chosen horse. Linc's horse gave him a hard time, and Carole insisted that he choose another horse. She couldn't afford to have the young riders on horses that gave them any trouble at all. Eventually, Linc decided on a horse that was so gray he was almost totally white. Linc seemed to think that meant he was sleek. Carole knew better. What it really meant was that he was old and in this case old seemed to mean gentle. Carole approved.

With a boost from Carole, the three campers mounted their horses. There was nobody to help Carole get onto Arthur's back, but fortunately he was patient and didn't seem to mind Carole's efforts. Finally, everybody was mounted up and the work began.

It didn't turn out to be much work at all, though. What happened was that Carole, on Arthur, led the way. As soon as Arthur began walking slowly back toward High Meadow, all the other horses simply followed. Carole had to be in front because she was on Arthur. The three campers brought up the rear. Clearly this was the accustomed position for Linc's tired old gray horse. As long as the three of them were pretty much walking abreast, Carole wasn't worried. If anything happened to one of them, there were two more to get her help.

Carole and the three bareback campers brought the herd into the pasture nearest the barn, and then Carole rode Arthur into his very own area. She dismounted, removed his bridle, and led the horse she'd mistaken for Arthur earlier back to the field with the rest of the herd.

Then all that remained was to help the campers dismount and remove their bridles. The job was quickly done.

Carole and the campers were going to return to the bunkhouse when they saw that the light was on in the kitchen of the main house. The four rustlers went to see what was going on. Inside they found a note from Jeannie and a plate of cookies. "Help yourself," the note said. "And sleep in tomorrow morning. Thank you all so much!"

"You mean we get a reward for stealing twenty horses?" Linc asked.

Carole laughed. "This time, Linc. Just this once."

Later Carole lay in bed, her mind filled with swirling thoughts. She felt very good about having gotten all the horses back to camp without the difficult neighbor's ever knowing about it. It was quite a victory, and she knew she was entitled to be proud. But at the same time, she'd caused the problem in the first place, and she didn't like that. It would have been a whole lot easier if she had done the right thing to begin with.

10

"THIS IS THE life, isn't it?" Stevie asked.

"I love it, too," Kate agreed.

The two of them were riding near one another at the back edge of a herd of obedient cattle. Eli was in the lead, twelve campers were strategically placed around the edge of the herd, and the two Saddle Club girls were on mop-up. Except that with Mel around there wasn't anything to mop up. She was a wonder to watch, apparently sensing trouble before it began. Mel didn't want a single steer or cow to get out of hand. She ran back and forth around the rear half of the herd and occasionally across the front of it—barking, growling, and wagging her tail busily, just to make her presence known.

"She's like an exam proctor," Kate observed. "The

kind who won't even let you tap your eraser just in case you're using Morse code."

"None of these dogies can get away with anything when she's around. By the way, what *is* a dogie?" Stevie asked.

"A motherless calf," Kate said. "They tend to be sort of directionless, so they need a lot of watching and guidance. That's where the expression 'Get along little dogies' comes from."

"I always thought it had something to do with puppies."

"Nope, cattle," Kate explained.

Suddenly, three steers shot out of the herd and headed to the left. Since Stevie was on the left, they were her responsibility. Kate stayed with the rest of the herd.

This sudden burst of activity seemed odd to Stevie, even though she knew that cattle sometimes behaved oddly. She also knew she could use some help. She whistled for Mel. Mel, however, was occupied with a pair that had gone off ahead of the rest of the herd and she couldn't be disturbed. Stevie signaled to two campers to give her a hand. They circled around the three errant steers and tried to convince them to get back with the herd.

The campers got two steers headed for the herd while Stevie chased after the third. By then the third one had made up his mind that he definitely didn't want to have anything to do with the pack. He'd just taken off.

Stevie took the rope off her saddle horn. She knew there was no way she could actually swing the thing around and capture the steer, but she thought that if she could get the fellow's attention by waving the rope, she could talk him into going away from her. The problem was, Stevie needed to be in *front* of the steer. Since the steer was running at full tilt, this was a true challenge.

Stevie thought about Stewball, the horse she'd ridden at Bar None. When it came to herding cattle, Stewball was as good as Mel. The horse she was riding today, an Appaloosa whose name she'd forgotten, was no Stewball. He seemed to need as much attention as the steer, and that was no help to Stevie. One thing about the horse, though, was that he was fast.

Finally, Stevie was able to get in front of the steer. She turned her horse around so he faced the oncoming animal. Her horse planted his feet in the ground. The steer stopped and did the same. It was like a game of chicken. If Stevie had been on Stewball, he would have known exactly how to dodge and block and keep the steer in check. This horse, however, needed Stevie to tell him what to do.

She used her legs, getting him to move to the left and right, along with the steer. Then she raised her hand, swung the rope around, and hollered. She didn't know why, she just thought it was a good idea. Her horse didn't know why she'd done it, either. It startled him so much that he bucked and then reared. Stevie wasn't prepared for that. She bounced in the air and landed flat on her bottom, right next to her horse. The good news was that her horse didn't run. The better news was that all the activity had convinced the steer he didn't want to proceed any farther afield. Calmly he turned and walked right back to the rest of the herd.

Stevie pulled herself up, rubbed the area that hurt the most, and then got back into the saddle. She found herself sitting on the area that hurt the most, but otherwise she was fine. She hoped nobody had seen her fall. She wasn't so lucky on that score.

"Nice flight!" said Lois.

"You forgot your cape, though," said Larry.

"Thanks, kids," said Stevie. "At least I got the steer back into the herd."

"Seemed to me that the steer did most of the work, dude," Larry said. Stevie did her best to shrug off the insult.

"Going's going to get tougher now," Eli said, circling back to the rear of the herd. "We're going to veer to the left and up that little hill."

"Doesn't look too bad," said Stevie.

"Wait'll you see the other side," said Eli. Then he noticed the dirt on her jeans. He didn't say anything.

Stevie thought she saw the smallest bit of a smile, but decided she was probably wrong. Eli wouldn't make fun of her. He knew she wasn't really a dude, didn't he? She didn't have a chance to say anything else, though, because Eli had to finish circling the herd and preparing all the cowboys for the turn and the hill.

The herd proceeded obediently up the incline, and then Stevie watched a curious thing. As each row of steer got to the top, they stopped, then proceeded down, almost jerking as they went. Stevie wondered what kind of landscape would cause that to happen so consistently.

Her question was answered when she and her horse reached the crest of the hill. She stopped and gaped. The hill was nearly straight down! There was a path and it was negotiable, but it was clearly treacherous. There would be no careful herding as the riders went down this hill. It would be everything they could do to manage the hill and stay on their horses.

"You okay, dude?" Larry asked her. The sneer was more than slight. "Don't forget to lean backwards," he said. "If you don't, you may fall off your horse. *Again*."

Stevie could think of a lot of retorts, but she found herself so worried that Larry might be right and she *might* fall off again that she just closed her mouth and kept all her retorts to herself. Fortunately, she made it to the bottom without mishap. So did all the campers. Not so the steer. There were eight or ten of them stuck on the hillside, frozen with fear and unable to move up or down. There was nothing to be done but to go get them. Eli got all the campers to circle the herd and told Stevie and Kate they'd have to help him with the frightened strays.

Stevie never minded work. She didn't even mind taking risks, like going back up the hill and working with the stray cattle. What she did mind was humiliation, which she was sure she'd get a big dose of on this mission. It looked like more than a little bit of trouble. The worst part was that every single camper would have a perfect view of whatever stupid thing she did.

"Stevie, this way!" Eli said, bringing her out of her reverie. The only thing worse than making a fool of herself would be being too afraid to try. She had to go. She went.

She and Kate caught up with Eli and picked their way back up the hill very carefully, watching their balance, and keeping an eye on the strays.

Each one of the strays presented a different challenge. One had a hoof lodged under a rock. All they had to do there was to pull the hoof out without getting crushed by the beefy creature or kicked by any of his other three working feet. Another two were just huddling together behind a tree, looking downward fearfully. Mel convinced them to move forward, parallel to the hillside, until there was no tree to protect them. Then they had no choice but to go downward. They did it and reached the bottom safely.

Another was a cow with a calf. There was nothing wrong with them except that the calf had decided this was the exact moment when he had to have lunch. While Eli, Kate, and Stevie watched, he finished nursing, and then he and his mother moved onward without any further prodding. Two of the strays needed to be talked down. Eli's system for that was to put a rope around the animal's neck and to get his horse to tug convincingly. Mel barked and snapped at the animal's feet while Stevie and Kate stood behind it and yelled encouragingly. Eventually, the strays decided that moving forward and downward was less unpleasant than being yanked, barked at, and yelled at.

The thought that kept going through Stevie's head as she and Kate worked with Eli was that there was no way in the world that she could have figured out how to do any of this without Eli there. Sure, she was staying on her horse, much to Larry's dismay, but it wasn't the same as really helping independently. Every time Eli figured out another way to solve the problems of the strays, Stevie felt dumber and more like a greenhorn dude.

Then, when the last stray was with the herd and they'd put that hill behind them and settled into a campsite for the night, Eli asked Stevie to build a camp fire. It was her final failure of the day. She could put all the ingredients exactly the way she thought they ought to be, but she couldn't get it to burn no matter what she did. Unfortunately, it was Lois who came to her rescue, adjusting the paper and the twigs until they were just so and then, with one match, got a roaring fire going.

Stevie and Kate didn't even stick around for the marshmallow roast. They headed for their bedrolls, hoping for a decent night's sleep on the hard cold ground. The other campers didn't even seem to notice or care that they weren't there. It was about what Stevie and Kate had come to expect.

STEVIE DIDN'T KNOW where she was when she first opened her eyes. She squinted in the gray light of dawn, barely making out the fact that there were kids in sleeping bags all around her. What clued her into her actual locale was the gentle and constant lowing sounds of the cattle nearby. She was on a cattle drive, and ever since the first hill, nothing had gone right.

She pulled herself out of her tent and looked at the surroundings. In spite of all the awful things that had happened yesterday, the place was nothing short of spectacular. They were in a valley, completely surrounded by the Rocky Mountains whose jagged, snowcapped tips reached into a pale blue-and-pink dawn. Stevie wondered how she could have missed the beauty of the place and then remembered that she'd had a few other things going on the previous day. She reminded herself to notice the beauty all day long today.

She stretched lazily, changed her clothes, washed up, and went in search of a way to be useful.

She found Eli laying a fire to cook breakfast. He asked her to finish doing it while he started closing up camp so they could get going quickly. Stevie laid the twigs, papers, and sticks out just the way she'd watched it being done before and put a match to the kindling. The kindling burned nicely, but the wood didn't catch fire at all. She tried again. No luck.

By the time she was ready to do it a third time, Kate had joined her and Eli had come to see what the problem was. He suggested that Stevie's talents would be better used getting the horses ready to be saddled up than smoldering kindling. Stevie wasn't sure if he was teasing or serious. It didn't improve her mood to start the day off with another failure.

"Be careful, though," he warned her. "Those animals are all kind of edgy this morning. I think there must be a coyote around. Just keep them all calm, okay?"

"Okay," Stevie and Kate agreed. The two of them walked together over to the temporary corral where their horses had been put for the night. The cattle milled around nearby, slightly restless as Eli had said they were.

When the girls got to the corral, they saw that the horses were a little restless, too. A couple of them had their ears laid way back on their heads, their eyes open so wide that they showed white.

"What's going on here?" Stevie asked.

"Eli must be right about the coyote," Kate said. "And nervousness is contagious. When one horse in a group gets edgy, all the others get it as well. Our best bet is just to show them we're not nervous."

"Great idea. The question is, how? Oh, I know!" Stevie was never happier than when she was being clever, and she'd come up with a clever idea to show she wasn't nervous. She began singing as she opened the gate to enter the corral. Apparently, however, she'd chosen a song the horses didn't much like. When she hit a high note and held it, one of the horses reared. The one next to it bucked, kicking another horse who bit the one who had reared. Every horse whose ears hadn't flattened before now flattened its ears, and they all started whinnying and crying wildly.

Two more horses reared, and that was all the rest of the herd would take. They fled.

Stevie and Kate stood helplessly by the open gate while more than a dozen horses raced past them right into the middle of the herd of cattle.

The cattle, which had been just as restless as the horses, found this an ideal opportunity to run. Within a matter of seconds it was clear to Stevie and Kate that they had a full-blown stampede on their hands.

"Eli!!!" Stevie shrieked, knowing then that making more noise couldn't possibly frighten the animals any more than they already were. She didn't really have to yell that loud, though. Eli had heard the frightened animals and was already on his way to help.

By the time he got there, the entire herd was in motion—a thousand animals running wildly through the valley. There wasn't a second to waste.

"Stevie! Get the campers to safety. Kate, come with me."

Stevie ran back to where the tents were pitched. For the moment, the herd was running away from the campsite, but she knew that could change on a second's notice. She didn't have to wake the campers up. The noise of the terrified herd had done that job for her. What she had to do was to keep them calm and get them to safety.

"As quickly as you can, put on your boots—don't worry about clean clothes now—roll up your beds, and come with me."

Lois came wandering out of her tent. "Help me comb my hair," she demanded.

"Later," Stevie said, firmly but kindly. "For now, just get ready to move."

Lois started to protest. This was no time to get into a tangle with a L-ion, but Stevie understood that sometimes, in a panic, people seem to feel the need to do very normal things, like combing their hair. "And be sure to bring your comb," Stevie said. "We'll do your hair as soon as we get resettled."

That seemed to be all the assurance Lois needed. She emerged from her tent a few seconds later, holding her bedroll and her comb. She had her boots on. Stevie paused only a split second to congratulate herself on motivating Lois properly.

"This way," she said, pointing to the hillside nearby. One thing the herd had learned yesterday was that they didn't like hills—up or down. Stevie thought that probably meant that even in a panic they wouldn't run up one. Also, that particular hillside had a couple of really good rocks on it that the kids could climb to safety where even the angriest steer would never follow.

"We're going to have a rock-climbing contest," Stevie said. "First one up to the top of that boulder gets a prize."

Stevie knew she wasn't fooling anyone with her ploy to get the campers to safety, but they all seemed reassured by the game.

"Last one up's a rotten egg," Larry said, leading the way. The kids scurried after him. No one wanted to let him win.

It took a lot of scrambling to get to the rock and a good deal more to get all the kids onto it. Stevie got them to work together, forming a sort of human chain so that the bigger kids could help the smaller ones up. Eventually twelve kids were safe and sound on a large boulder overlooking a valley where a herd of cattle, mingled with horses, was running wildly. They were so proud of the way they'd gotten up that they even forgot to notice who the last one—the rotten egg—was. It was Stevie, of course. She had to be last to be sure that the kids were all safe before she joined them.

"Come on, Lois, let me comb your hair now," Stevie said. Lois seemed surprised that Stevie was as good as her word, but she also seemed comforted to have the job done. Stevie made a French braid for Lois, and two other girls thought she'd done such a neat job of it that they wanted her to do it to their hair as well. Even the boys were impressed with Stevie's skill and watched in rapt attention at her ministrations.

All the while, Stevie was acutely aware of the chaos in the valley below. As soon as the kids were totally calm, she could give Eli and Kate a hand.

She thought it was a good idea to give the campers something to occupy themselves. She explained that she was going to help Eli and Kate.

"Will you be safe?" Larry interrupted her. Stevie was touched by the obvious concern in his voice. Less than twelve hours earlier, he would have been delighted if somebody had told him Stevie had drowned in a creek.

"I'll be safe," she assured him. "And Eli and Kate will be safer. They need me, too. So, while I'm gone, I want the twelve of you to play a game and make up a story." She quickly explained the rules. "Okay here goes: A long time ago, there was a mean old hermit who lived under a boulder on a hillside overlooking a valley in the Rockies. He hated everybody. He *especially* hated children. And *then* . . ."

She looked at Larry to take over. He began right away. "One day a little girl was skipping and hopping across the valley . . ."

Stevie knew the kids would be just fine. It was time for her to get to Kate and Eli. As the story progressed to the point at which the hermit sneaked an ugly toad in the basket the little girl was carrying, Stevie scrambled back down the rock and onto the valley floor where things were not so calm.

At first it was hard to see how Stevie could do anything to help. Then just the thing she needed arrived by her side: a horse.

Without a saddle and bridle, she might have some trouble controlling the animal, but the roan gelding was standing still near her, clearly relieved to have stopped running. Stevie thought that, like the children, he was really just waiting for somebody in authority to tell him what to do. Stevie grabbed a handful of his mane and jumped upward onto his high back. It took two tries, but she was soon aboard, and the horse's ears flicked alertly. He waited for instructions.

Stevie didn't make him wait very long. She got him into a lope—what Western riders called cantering—and took him across the valley floor to where Eli and Kate, with the help of Mel, were trying to subdue the herd.

"Kids okay?" Eli asked when he saw Stevie. Both he and Kate were mounted bareback, without bridles, the same as Stevie. Three great minds with a single thought, she realized. They had to be on horseback, no matter what.

"Fine," she said. "What about the cattle?"

"See for yourself."

Stevie looked. The cattle were still running, but more slowly.

"They just get tired," Eli said. "They slow down."

"So it's over?" she asked.

"Not yet," said Eli. "The same thing that started them in the first place could start them all over again. And the only thing worse than panicked cattle running wild is tired, panicked cattle. They make even less sense."

"The same thing won't start them again," Stevie assured him. "It was me, singing."

Eli shook his head. Stevie felt the full weight of his

disappointment at her. It was hard to think that his disapproval could make her feel any worse than she already did, but it had that effect. She felt awful. Then Eli spoke.

"I don't think so, Stevie. I've heard you sing and though it won't get you into the Metropolitan Opera, it's not all that scary. These creatures heard a coyote howl. You just didn't hear it because you were singing."

"You think so?"

He didn't have time to answer the question, though. Because precisely at that moment, the herd began running again. This time, though, instead of running away from the campsite, they turned and ran straight toward it!

"Let's get out of here!" Kate said, realizing that the entire herd was aimed right at them and there was no stopping them. The three of them dashed out of the way, knowing they couldn't do anything right then, except save themselves.

Mel wasn't so convinced of that fact, however, and she definitely didn't like the idea that all those cattle were disobeying her at once. She barked wildly and growled. She even snapped at the passing legs. Then, while Eli, Kate, and Stevie watched in horror, Mel completely disappeared in the sea of racing cattle, and then they could no longer hear her barking.

"Mel!" Eli cried out. Eli loved that dog and

couldn't stand the idea that something might happen to her.

Kate covered her eyes. Stevie felt the tears rise. "No!" she cried. It couldn't be true!

The herd moved across the valley, like a thundering blanket, with the animals' backs making a solid throbbing brown mass. As they neared the campsite, they veered to the left, saving most of what was there, except for one tent that got mangled by a thousand legs running over it. Then the herd was completely past the three riders and completely past the campsite and there was still no sign of Mel.

And as suddenly as it had started running, the herd stopped, drawing to a halt. The animals looked around at one another in apparent surprise. The horses separated themselves from the cattle, milling around the edge of the herd of cattle. A few of the steers glanced at the grassy earth beneath their feet and took a bite. Others sniffed the air, curiously, and turned toward the creek. They sauntered over to the fresh water and took a drink.

"Is it over?" Kate asked Eli, astonished at the abruptness of the halt.

"Almost," he said. His eyes never left the herd. There was one question that hadn't been answered: Mel.

Then they heard it—the sound they had each been praying to hear. It was Mel's bark. She dashed out from between the legs of the cattle, turned, lowered her front legs as if preparing to pounce in case anybody gave her one more ounce of trouble and barked. The cattle stared at her blankly. They looked as if they were wondering what the dog was making a fuss about. They were standing still, after all. Wasn't that what she wanted?

Then, secure in the knowledge that her job was done, Mel turned and trotted easily to where Eli sat bareback on his horse. She looked up at him for approval and then lay down, too tired to go another step.

Eli slid off the back of his horse and gathered the brave dog in his arms. Without a word, he carried her to his tent. She needed a rest and she would get it.

The rest of the day was in sharp contrast to the morning. Eli took his rifle and went in search of the animal that had frightened the cattle so badly. He never found it and in spite of all the trouble the predator had apparently caused, Stevie was relieved that Eli hadn't had to shoot anything. Kate put herself in charge of cleaning up the campsite and setting up the tent that had been knocked down. When that was done, she rounded up the rest of the horses and put them back in the corral from which they'd exited so abruptly that morning.

Stevie went to the rock to fetch the campers. By

the time she got there, each of them had contributed to the story and the tale had taken a rather odd twist that seemed to have the hermit living in Santa Claus's house while taking a correspondence course on how to fix cellular telephones. Stevie didn't want to know how he'd gotten there, but she felt a great deal of pride in the fact that they were still playing the game she'd started them on a few hours earlier.

Together the twelve campers and Stevie reversed their ascent onto the boulder, each child helping another get down. Together, the twelve of them, and their counselor, returned to the campsite, now somewhat reassembled. It was afternoon by then and the only thing that made sense was to stay at the campsite for another night before taking the final leg of their journey with the herd. Their destination was on the other side of the row of hills at the far end of the valley. They'd get there by evening tomorrow. For now, they all needed rest. That was as true of the people as it was of the animals.

Stevie suggested to the kids that they might want to go take a cooling swim in the creek. They all went into their tents to find their bathing suits. Stevie and Kate put theirs on, too. Before they joined the kids for a swim, however, they stepped into Eli's tent. They wanted to check on Mel.

The dog lay on her side, her eyes closed, breathing evenly. Her face twitched.

"Is she in pain?" Stevie asked Eli who was sitting nearby watching every move.

"I don't think so," Eli said. "I checked her over pretty carefully and I don't think she got hurt at all, though I can't imagine how that could be. She's just dreaming. You know how it is. When something really exciting happens, you tend to dream about it. I think she's dreaming about barking at running cattle. It's her kind of dream, you know."

"I know," Stevie said. She reached out and patted the sleeping dog ever so gently. It seemed like a very small gesture of thanks to a dog who had single-pawedly quelled a stampede.

"You all go swimming now," Eli said. "Then we'll have something to eat and a good night's sleep. We've earned it. We'll finish the drive tomorrow. I'm going to stay here with Mel a few minutes more. Go on ahead."

The swim in the creek felt wonderful. The dinner they made tasted delicious, and Stevie thought that nothing had ever felt better than being in her own sleeping bag, looking up at the brightly sparkling stars and sleeping. Her last thought before she went to sleep was to wonder if her face would twitch the way Mel's had while she slept. Barking at stampeding cattle might just be her kind of dream that night, too!

CAROLE PATTED HER back pocket, wanting to be sure the letter was still there. It had arrived the day before, covered all over with funny-looking stamps and postmarks. It was from Lisa and she was in Italy. Carole had wanted nothing more than to tear it open and read it right then, but she thought it was only fair to wait until Kate and Stevie got back from the cattle drive. It was addressed to The Saddle Club and reading it out loud would be a sort of Saddle Club meeting for the three of them when Stevie and Kate arrived.

Things had been quiet at the ranch, once Arthur was alone in his field and the other horses were in theirs. Linc, Ellis, and Jack had been relatively cooperative since their "rustling" experience. Carole had taken advantage of their new mode of behavior to teach them everything she could about riding. At first, they'd been more than a little reluctant to learn anything about what they thought of as "sissy" riding, but when Carole showed them what she could do with a horse and an English saddle, they'd changed their minds a little. They weren't ready to sign up for dressage lessons, but they began to have a little respect for the finer points of equitation and jumping. One of them, Ellis, even acknowledged that Pony Club might be almost as much fun as his 4-H Club. Carole took that as high praise and didn't push her luck. "Could be," she said.

Now the days of emptiness at High Meadow were over. The cattle drive was complete, although a day longer than expected, for some reason Carole didn't know, and her friends would be returning.

Carole was pulling weeds from around the carrots when she saw Kate, Stevie, and Eli approach, accompanied by twelve campers. Mel was at the head of the group, leading the way. Everyone there was dusty, dirty, and looked very tired.

"Where's the nearest shower?" Stevie asked.

"This way, but I'm first," said Kate, pointing at their bunkhouse.

Normally Carole would have reminded her friends that, actually, it was the horses who came first, but in this case, she considered it wise to make an exception. Clearly the cowpokes needed a break. She rounded up

Linc, Ellis, and Jack to help take care of the horses and told everybody else to go clean up and get a little rest. Jeannie announced that dinner would be ready in an hour. Carole told her friends there would be a Saddle Club meeting after that.

"I'll do anything you tell me," Stevie said, "as long as it starts with a shower."

Carole had the feeling that there was a good long story to the cattle drive, and she was eager to hear it. And she had some things to tell Stevie and Kate about, too. First, though, she and the three campers took care of the horses, took off their tack, gave them a brushing and some fresh water, and set them loose in the field with the rest of the horses. They seemed to enjoy their reunion as well.

Then Carole returned to the kitchen to help Jeannie finish dinner preparations. It was another couple of hours before the Saddle Club girls had any time together. By then all the stories had been told and everybody was ready for bed.

The girls retreated to their bunkhouse.

"I've got a surprise," Carole said mysteriously.

"Something good?" Stevie asked. "I hope so, because I can't take another dose of bad news now."

"Really good," Carole said. She reached in her back pocket and pulled out Lisa's letter. "It's another letter from Lisa!"

"What's the news?" Stevie asked eagerly.

"I don't know. I haven't read it yet," Carole said as she carefully opened the envelope.

"Only you," Stevie said. She would have read the letter right away herself.

Carole unfolded the several sheets, held them to the dim light in the cabin, and began reading.

Dear Carole, Kate, and Stevie, and Eli, and Jeannie, too,

I'm getting to like traveling in Europe. In fact, it seems that the more I get to like it, the less my parents get to like it. That's pretty strange. Of course, that doesn't mean I don't wish I were with you guys. I do. I really do! Especially since you guys already know what you're doing. I'm learning something new every day.

"Shows how much she knows!" Stevie joked.

"Even more, it shows how *little* we know," said Kate.

Carole continued reading.

I'm writing to you from Italy now.

Today we drove through the area known as Tuscany. It's just beautiful here. Very hilly (though nothing compared to the Rockies, but you know what I mean). There are little towns tucked in the hillsides with old old houses that have orange tile roofs. It's something.

We stopped in a small town to get some lunch and fill up our tank with gas. It's a good thing we don't do that much—gas is over $6 a gallon, if I've done my math correctly. Mom and Dad kept looking at the menu and couldn't make any sense of it. Naturally, I had my phrase book handy. They told me what they wanted and I ordered it for them. They seemed pretty grateful. The waiter was really impressed. Honestly, so was I. I'm actually getting good at it—thumbing through the phrase book, I mean, not speaking Italian!

That's not what I really wanted to tell you about though. The really fantastic thing happened later.

After lunch Dad went and found a telephone. He wanted to call the hotel to make sure our reservation was okay. Mom went with him. They took the phrase book with them. While they were away from the table, I got into a conversation with a woman at the table next to us. I was wearing my Saddle Club pin and she noticed it. She spoke a little English; I spoke a little Italian. We made out okay.

What I realized as we started talking was that she was actually wearing riding clothes! It took two or three times around the vocabulary list for me to realize that she was asking me if my parents and I were attending the horse show in the next town. Can you believe it? There was actually a horse show going on and I didn't know it until she told me.

Well, of course, I just had to go. Mom had been talking about some ancient ruin, but what's an ancient ruin compared to a horse show? I didn't think I'd have too much trouble convincing Dad, because he'd had it up to here with ancient ruins. I was all ready to do my convincing talk when the looks on their faces told me there was trouble.

It turned out that the hotel at which we had a reservation was totally booked because of the horse show. My parents had gone all through the phrase book, looking for a way to threaten to sue. The best they could do was to get a promise from the hotel that, if we showed up there, they'd see what they could do to find us a place to stay.

Since it was my idea to get to the horse show anyway, I thought that was fine. We paid our bill and drove on over to the hotel. My parents were very upset. I guess I can't blame them, but I was pretty sure something would work out. It's always seemed to me that when there were horses around, everything else worked out. Know what I mean?

Kate grunted. Stevie laughed. Carole went on reading.

So, while they went to try to sweet talk the hotel into finding a place for us to stay, I walked on over to the horse show. It was practically across the street.

I bought a ticket, got a program that I hardly understood, and just walked around. Everything was outdoors. There were about four rings with events going on all at the same time. I watched a dressage exhibition in the main ring and watched a preliminary jumping event in a smaller ring. It was really fun. I missed you guys, though, because there wasn't anybody for me to talk to. Even if my parents had been there (and they were still at the hotel then), they wouldn't have understood what they were watching. Mom judges horses by their looks and their pedigrees, rather than by their performance, and Dad tends to want to know how much money they're going to win and who is betting on them—that is if he's not preoccupied with where he's going to eat his next meal.

ANYWAY—this is the really interesting, nearly unbelievable, but absolutely true part. I wandered over to the area where the junior competitors were having their events. They were doing hunter jumping and they were pretty good. There was one boy who was far and away better than any of the rest of them. I was really impressed. He went through the first round with flying colors and then when he brought his horse out for the conformation judging, I couldn't believe my eyes.

Enrico. It was actually Enrico. Remember him?

"Enrico? You mean like one of the Italian boys?" Stevie asked.

"I guess so," said Carole.

"Incredible!" said Stevie. Enrico was one of the four Italian boys who had come to Pine Hollow. Stevie remembered how Lisa had said she might run into them and how she and Carole had laughed at the idea. Now, it seemed it had actually come true. It amazed Stevie and Carole. Out of all the millions of people in Italy, their friend Lisa had just happened to run into one of the four Italian citizens she actually knew!

I didn't want to upset him during the judging, but as soon as he brought his horse over to the side of the ring, I started yelling and waving. I only made a slight idiot of myself before he saw me. He told me to wait right there—until the ribbons were handed out. Of course, he got a blue. Then he came over and gave me this most gigantic hug. He asked me what I was doing there and how you guys are and what was going on and everything. I couldn't answer all his questions at once, but the minute I told him about the hotel, he got this wonderful look on his face.

"But you and your parents—you will stay with us!"

"You have room for all of us?" I asked. He told me that of course he did. Little did I know.

Right then my parents showed up. They were as mad as could be and Dad was on the verge of saying all sorts of things about Italian innkeepers. I introduced them to Enrico and told them we had a place to stay.

I won't bore you with all the details now—I'll have months and months to do that when I get home—but I will tell you that as I write this, I'm sitting at an antique Italian secretary (that's a fancy word for a small desk) in Enrico's family mansion. This isn't just a house. Oh, it also turned out that the horse show wasn't being given in any funky old public park. It was being given on Enrico's family estate. I mean estate. It goes on for acres and acres and it's been in his family for many generations. My parents and I are in our very own wing or something. I'm not sure exactly because the place is just too big for me to be completely oriented. I do know that when we want *breakfast, we're supposed to ring for a servant who will either bring it to us or show us the way to the dining room. I'm telling you, you've never seen anything like this.*

Now I think I'll take a bath. The bathtub is about the size of a small swimming pool. Of course, the one in my parents' bathroom is much larger. . . .

Just kidding. Still it's all pretty grand.

It's hard to believe this vacation is almost over. It's been so interesting. When I think about it, before I left, I was scared to death about being in unfamiliar places with unfamiliar languages. I've realized that people are people, and if you try to be nice and try to speak to them in their own language, no matter how badly you mangle the phrases from the phrase book, they want to be helpful and welcoming. I've enjoyed the trip. I'm a little sorry it's almost over, but I can't wait to see you guys and hear everything about High Meadow. I get to read your diaries, right? Don't leave anything out!

Love,
Lisa

Stevie looked at Carole. "Have you included everything in your diary?" she asked.

"Almost," Carole said. "Well, not exactly. No,

come to think of it, there are a few things I've overlooked. Intentionally."

"It won't make any difference," Stevie said. "She'll find out anyway."

"How will she find out?" Kate asked.

"We'll tell her, of course," said Carole. "We just don't have any secrets." But considering the way their experience as ranch hands was going, she sort of wished they did.

13

THE SADDLE CLUB girls managed to get through the last
week at High Meadow without any obvious disasters.
That seemed to Stevie to be somewhat of a victory.
There were no more stampedes or wandering herds of
horses. None of the kids got badly hurt, though Linc
skinned his knee when he got thrown from a horse
trying to jump in a Western saddle. By the last day,
the girls thought they pretty much had the routine
down. Though it didn't seem right that it had taken
that long to do it.

At dinner that night, when they were eating their
last plates of trail stew (Eli's specialty), Eli announced
there would be a special camp fire at 9 P.M. They
should all come in pajamas and bathrobes and bring
their sleeping bags for warmth.

Nights at High Meadow could get quite cool. That made for very good sleeping weather, as long as your sleeping bag was cozy. After dinner and cleanup, the girls donned their sweatpants and sweatshirts—preferred sleeping garb for cold nights—and their woolly slippers and headed for the camp fire.

Flames danced upward, brightly reaching toward the starry sky from what appeared to be more like a bonfire than a camp fire. Jeannie handed out marshmallows, graham crackers, and chocolate squares.

"S'mores!" Stevie shouted excitedly. A few of the kids had never had them. Stevie, Carole, and Kate explained exactly how to make the perfect one.

"You have to get the marshmallow gooey enough to melt the chocolate bar when you make the cookie sandwich," Kate said.

"You mean I can't just burn the thing?" Lois asked.

"Only if you want to eat charcoal," Kate told her.

At Kate's insistence Lois tried for golden brown. It wasn't easy in the bonfire, but she succeeded more or less, and when she'd assembled her snack and bitten into it, she declared s'mores to be one of Mother Nature's most nearly perfect foods. Nobody disputed that.

Eli stood up to talk to the group then. It occurred to Stevie that he'd waited until everybody's mouth was full so they couldn't interrupt him. He cleared his throat.

"It's hard to believe that our time here is over and that tomorrow you all will be leaving to go back to your homes," he began. He spoke about how much fun he and Jeannie had with all of them and how he hoped all the campers would want to come back next year.

Except for us, Stevie thought ruefully.

"A lot of things went wrong at first," Eli said.

Everything went wrong at first, Stevie thought. And at second and at third . . .

"But eventually, we got it all going and I think everybody had a good time and learned something. I know I did and Jeannie did, too."

Yeah, like you wish you'd never invited The Saddle Club, thought Stevie.

"I want to thank you all for being a part of High Meadow's first year. I especially want to thank three of you for pitching in and getting things done even when you didn't know what you were getting done."

He probably means the L-ions. They were more use than we were.

"Of course I mean Kate, Carole, and Stevie—"

"Yeah!" said one of the kids, who then began clapping. Ellis patted Carole on the back. Larry shook Kate's hand. Two campers waved proudly at Stevie.

"It would have been a very different summer without you three—"

"Right, like there wouldn't have been a stampede,

126

you mean?" Stevie asked, this time expressing her thoughts out loud.

Eli laughed. "Maybe so," he said. "But in my experience if that hadn't happened, something else would have. Besides, nobody got hurt, though one of our tents is a little the worse for wear, and the campers keep telling me about this neat story they made up while you and Kate and I were helping Mel calm the herd. So? It happened and we solved the problem. We even got the herd where it was supposed to go, just a day late."

The girls could barely believe their ears. They'd really thought Eli and Jeannie had been disappointed in them, and now here they were telling everybody in public what a wonderful job they'd done. Was he just being nice?

"There's another thing, too," Eli said. "Jeannie and I were talking about it last night. See, we knew when we decided to have this camp that a lot of things were going to go wrong. We figured we'd cause most of them ourselves and feel bad about it and then we wouldn't know how to get out of the messes we caused. That's what made us decide to invite you girls to come along. We knew that if you were here, you'd be the ones to cause the trouble and you would also find much better ways than we ever could of solving the problems. Boy, were we right!"

The campers all laughed. So did Eli and Jeannie. So

did the girls. It was Eli's way of saying they'd made trouble, all right, but everything had come out fine in the end, and that was what mattered.

Eli pulled out a guitar then and handed it to Jeannie. She began strumming it softly, and the songs began. It was a little corny to be sitting around a camp fire on a star-studded night, surrounded by mountains and meadows, singing cowboy songs. In fact it was so corny that it was perfect. Everybody joined in. The strains of the guitar and their voices seemed to reach up to the mountains and the sky, filling the night with music.

Then there was another sound in the distance, at first a mere hum and then more distinct. It was the sound of an airplane.

Kate smiled, knowing that it was her father. Frank Devine had found an airstrip nearby and had flown in to take her and her friends out early the following morning.

Camp was over. It was time to go home.

14

"LEEEEEESSAAA!" Stevie shrieked the minute she spotted her friend walking up the drive at Pine Hollow. "Come on, Carole, she's home!"

The three girls met in front of the stable and exchanged big hugs. They hadn't seen one another for more than four weeks. It had seemed like a lifetime.

"Time for a Saddle Club meeting," Lisa said. "But first of all, I've got to get back onto a horse. I haven't ridden in a month!"

"Unless you count that little hack you took in Windsor," Stevie teased.

"Oh, right, that. And then there was the ride I took with Enrico while we were staying at his 'cottage.' But still, it wasn't as much riding as I would have done if

I'd been here or with you. Let's ride to the creek and talk there."

That sounded just about perfect to Stevie and Carole. It only took the girls a few minutes to tack up their horses and get permission to go on a trail ride. Mrs. Reg didn't bother to ask where they were going. She knew they just wanted a chance to talk and catch up. She said it was fine.

When the horses were ready, the girls mounted them and then each touched the good-luck horseshoe to guarantee a safe return. They were off.

At first, as they rode, it almost seemed as if there were so much to say that they couldn't say anything. Each of them was so happy, once again, to be on her own favorite horse, riding at her own favorite place, that words couldn't begin to capture the feeling. Carole led them in a trot and then a canter across the field to the woods.

It was a muggy hot Virginia day. The sun beat down on them, bringing beads of sweat under their riding helmets. The pungent scent of warm horses cut through the air and filled their noses. As far as they were concerned, it was just about perfect.

When they reached the woods, Carole slowed Starlight to a walk, to let him cool down in the shady cover. The girls began talking then.

"That was incredible about running into Enrico!" Stevie said.

"It sure was. He was so nice to us, too. And his parents were just wonderful. They promised to come visit us sometime. My parents didn't seem too thrilled about that, though—not that they didn't like Enrico's parents. It's just that our nice little four-bedroom house hardly seems like a fair exchange for their manor house! Wow, I mean, I've got to tell you about that place."

"You sure do," Carole agreed.

"But first, you guys have to tell me about High Meadow. Was it wonderful?"

Carole and Stevie looked at one another. That was a good question. *Was it wonderful?* It had been hard. It had been confusing. It had been trying. The campers had given them a tough time. The routines were difficult to get used to. *Wonderful?*

"Yes," Stevie said, finally. "It *was* wonderful. It just didn't seem that way all the time."

Lisa looked at her friends. That wasn't the answer she'd expected.

"Do you remember that story Mrs. Reg told us before we left on our trips about the boy who wanted to be a jockey and ended up being a trainer?"

Both Carole and Lisa recalled it.

"I think I know what it was about now. She was trying to warn us that our expectations were going to turn out to be all out of whack, but that it would work out in the end in a way that would be even better than our expectations."

Carole felt mildly annoyed, not because she thought Stevie was wrong, but because she realized she was right. "How is it Mrs. Reg always knows what's going to happen to us?"

Stevie smiled and shook her head. "Beats me."

"What's going on here?" Lisa asked. "What *did* happen at High Meadow? Am I going to have to read every word of your diaries to get a few simple answers to a few simple questions?"

"My diary would be short reading," Stevie said. "You know me, don't you?"

"Sure," Lisa said. "I bet you made one long entry the night before you left for High Meadow, a medium length entry the first night you got there, before anything happened, and then two scribbled one-sentence entries much later on. Right?"

"Wrong," Stevie said. "I didn't do the medium length one. Just the one long and the two scribbled."

Lisa wasn't surprised. That was just like Stevie. She hoped she could count on Carole, though.

"Not much better," Carole told her. "I did a couple of entries that you're welcome to read, but on the worst days, I didn't write anything. Stevie and I are just going to have to tell you everything that happened."

"Everything?" Stevie asked, still uncomfortable

about confessing every dumb thing she, Carole, and Kate had done in the three weeks at High Meadow.

"Everything," Carole said. "And I know just the place to do it."

She drew Starlight to a halt and dismounted. They had arrived at the creek, and they had a routine there that they followed whenever the weather allowed it. Today's weather was perfect for it.

The girls secured their horses to branches of the trees that stood by the creek so the horses could get fresh water. Then they removed their own riding boots and socks and climbed onto a flat rock that overhung the stream. They each hiked up their pants and let their feet dangle in the water.

"Nothing ever felt so good!" Carole declared.

"Oh, I'm not sure about that," said Stevie. "The swim after the stampede was pretty terrific."

"*Stampede?*" Lisa said.

That seemed like as good a place as any to begin.

By the time Carole and Stevie finished telling all, Lisa was laughing. It was the one reaction they hadn't expected from their friend.

"You certainly kept everybody busy, didn't you? And you finally tamed the L-ions. Did you really get Linc to jump?"

"Yes, I did," Carole said, a little proudly. "He didn't want to admit that he liked doing it. He kept saying he wanted to try it to prove how sissy English jumping was, but then he seemed to want to try it a lot. I'm sure he liked it."

"And, you, Stevie, finding a way to keep twelve kids quiet and calm in the middle of a stampede! No wonder Eli thought you guys were so great!"

"We didn't think he did," Carole said.

"As I remember Eli, he has a way of keeping his thoughts to himself, doesn't he?"

"Sure," said Stevie. "What I forgot, though, was that if he's angry about something, he'll let you know. I should have realized that when he wasn't angry, he must have been pleased. It would have saved me a lot of worrying."

That didn't sound like it made sense, but Carole agreed with it because she knew it was right.

Lisa swirled her feet in the cool water and watched the ripples reflect the trees and sky above. "You know, I was thinking," she began. "At first, it was hard being away from home, but I got used to it. When we left, I was terribly afraid of all the things I didn't know, but I found that what I did know was enough. That made me feel good."

"And when we left home, we were just full of ourselves, very sure that all the stuff we knew would be more than enough. It didn't turn out that way. We had to learn a lot more and prove ourselves to the campers, Eli, and Jeannie. Mostly to ourselves, though, I guess," Carole said.

"Being away from home is hard sometimes," Stevie observed. "Even when you're glad to be where you are."

"Right," Carole mused.

"But being away from home wasn't as hard as being away from my friends," said Lisa. "I missed Willow Creek and Pine Hollow, but most of all I missed The Saddle Club."

"Well, we're all back together again now!" Stevie announced, as if she'd just realized the significance of their trail ride. "And like Dorothy says in *The Wizard of Oz*, 'There's no place like home!' "

"Especially if 'home' is a stable!" said Lisa. Then she reached over and took a handful of water and splashed it on her two friends. Stevie and Carole weren't sure what felt so wonderful about that—the cool water dripping down their hot faces or the fact that their best friend Lisa had splashed it on them. They decided not to waste any more time thinking about that. Instead, they decided to retaliate. In seconds, creek water was splashing all over the place.

The Saddle Club was back together.

About the Author

BONNIE BRYANT is the author of more than fifty books for young readers, including novelizations of movie hits such as *Teenage Mutant Ninja Turtles® and Honey, I Blew Up the Kid*, written under her married name, B.B. Hiller.

Ms. Bryant began writing The Saddle Club in 1986. Although she had done some riding before that, she intensified her studies then and found herself learning right along with her characters Stevie, Carole, and Lisa. She claims that they are all much better riders than she is.

Ms. Bryant was born and raised in New York City. She lives in Greenwich Village with her two sons.